Other se

G000093399

This dangerously handsom   o's foremost paranormal inves..g..... w.... magical aptitude and specialized weapons, Luther Cross will handle your supernatural problems… for the right price.

THE MYTH HUNTER

All the legends of the world have some element of truth to them. And to track down those legends, there are the myth hunters. Some, like Elisa Hill, are explorers, trying to learn more about the world. And some are soldiers of fortune, whose only goal is profit and exploitation, no matter the risk.

INFERNUM

A shadowy, globe-spanning network of operatives run by the mysterious power broker known as Dante. They hold allegiance to no one, existing as rogues on the fringes of society. No matter the job, Infernum has an operative to execute it—provided you have the means to pay for it!

VANGUARD

The world has changed. A mysterious event altered the genetic structure of humanity, granting a small percentage of the population superhuman powers. A small team of these specials has been formed to deal with potential threats. Paragon—telekinetic powerhouse; Zenith—hyper-intelligent automaton; Shift—shape-changing teenager; Wraith—teleporting shadow warrior; Sharkskin—human/shark hybrid. Led by the armored Gunsmith, they are Vanguard!

Visit PercivalConstantine.com for an up-to-date list of titles!

Published by Pulp Corner Press

http://www.percivalconstantine.com

A MORNINGSTAR NOVEL

LUCIFER JUDGED

BY PERCIVAL CONSTANTINE

CHAPTER 1

A flash of pure, blue light appeared in the night sky above the shore of Lake Michigan. The light quickly took shape and slowly faded as it transformed into a beautiful woman with long, dark hair, piercing blue eyes, and feathered wings wrapped around her body. The angel named Anael unfurled her wings and they gently lowered her to the surface of the water, where she was able to set her feet down as if she were standing on solid ground.

Her wings folded back and the feathers emitted a soft, azure glow. The wings receded into her back and once they were gone, so was the illumination. Anael walked across the water's surface and came to the edge, stepping onto the soft sand.

This part of the lake bordered Evanston's Lakeshore Historic District. The homes here were large mansions, bordering areas of far more economic distress. A perfect microcosm of humanity—those with the means to help ignoring the problems right in front of them.

Anael hadn't come here for a stroll along the lakefront, nor to admire the beauty of the excessive mansions. She was here to visit one home in particular, and to tell the occupant that she was well and truly done with him once and for all.

That might have sounded dramatic, if it were the first time Anael had done such a thing. But she felt it was starting to become a pattern with the man she had once loved and pledged her soul to. He had promise once, but he threw it all away. And in her attempts to try to help him find his way back, she herself was now a pariah. She hadn't even tried to return to Heaven yet, so fearful was she of what the reactions would be once she did set foot in the capital city of Elysium.

The Tudor-style mansion was just across the road from the lake. The streets were empty, and yet Anael still found herself hesitating before crossing the distance. She took a deep breath and then set a foot off the curb. Her steps were slow and methodical, but soon, she had reached the front door. When she raised her hand to press the doorbell, her finger just hovered over the button.

"This is stupid…" she chastised herself and then pressed it.

She could hear the melodic ringing of the chimes from behind the door and she waited for a few moments. When no answer came, she pressed the button a second time. It was then that the door finally opened and she looked up into the face of a man with broad shoulders, a shaved head, and yellow eyes.

"Thank you for coming," said Belial.

"Might be too soon for gratitude," said Anael. "I haven't agreed to anything yet."

"Come in." Belial held the door open for her and Anael stepped inside.

She was somewhat taken aback by the demon's manner.

Normally, theirs was an antagonistic relationship and they had exchanged blows on more than one occasion. In this very house, in fact. But now, he was extremely cordial—almost deferential. She found herself missing the animosity.

As Belial led her through the house, she was surprised to see two unfamiliar figures sitting in the library. Anael stopped to examine them and the pair turned their heads in synchronous movements to look at her. They were dressed in identical black suits with leather gloves and sunglasses. One was completely bald and rail-thin. The other was stockier with straggly hair framing his face and a full beard. They weren't demons, nor were they human. Anael couldn't quite a sense of *what* exactly they were. But something about them both unnerved her.

"A condition of Lucifer's 'bail,' for lack of a better term," said Belial. "Consider them court-appointed monitors."

"Who are they?" she asked. "For that matter, *what* are they?"

"Their names are Grant and Moore," said Belial. "As for what they are…that's more difficult to answer. They're agents of Purgatory and that's all anyone really knows of them. This way."

Belial led her away from the library and down the corridor to the kitchen.

"I don't understand. Why is Purgatory involved in this?"

"They're not, but they serve as a neutral third party. The Court was divided on whether or not the Morningstar could be allowed free on his own recognizance and any monitors proposed by one camp would be seen as suspect by the other."

"No honor among demons?"

Belial ignored her jab and just opened the door in the kitchen that led to the patio. "He's in the pool."

Anael walked through the door and stepped out onto the wooden deck. There was a staircase that led down to the ground level, where an in-ground pool sat. The lights beneath the water illuminated the blue-painted concrete, and the silhouette of a man swam laps from one end to the other.

She walked down the steps, keeping her eyes on his form. Once she reached the foot of the stairs, Anael stepped up to the pool's edge. He didn't stop to acknowledge her, just continued swimming. But on the final lap, he didn't swim to the end of the pool, instead coming towards her. He sunk beneath the water and Anael was surprised to see a bright light emerging from beneath the surface. The pool started to bubble, as if it were boiling. Anael stepped back and watched in surprise, the percolation intensifying. And then his head pierced the surface, his body rising from the pool in full defiance of gravity, with large wings spread out behind him. When he opened his eyes, they were yellow and burning as bright as the afternoon sun.

He hovered above the water and his wings carried him over to the pool's edge. His bare feet touched down and his wings receded into his back. Rings of flame-like energy encircled his body, forging clothing over his naked form. The energy dissipated and Lucifer stood before Anael, wearing a smile on his face.

"It's good to see you, Ana," he said.

"Hardly the words I'd expect after our last encounter," said Anael. "I see you managed to get your powers back. So returning to Hell did the trick, huh?"

"Not without some challenges along the way," said

Lucifer. "Since you're here, I take it Mara delivered the message?"

"She did," said Anael. "And I have to say, I'm pretty confused."

"About what?"

"Try everything."

Lucifer gave a chuckle and walked over to a table with a bottle of brandy resting on top with two glasses. He sat in one of the deck chairs and gestured for Anael to take the other. She remained standing. Lucifer just shrugged and poured himself a drink.

"My actions started all of this. Humanity's awakening, the war, eons of conflict, Cocytus—it can all be traced back to a decision I made long ago," said Lucifer. "And so my guilt is going to be judged by the people of Hell."

"And what's the charge?" asked Anael.

"Conspiring against them by working in concert with the Divine Choir."

Anael scoffed. "You weren't working with the Choir, you were working *against* them."

"Was I?" asked Lucifer. "Every good story requires a good villain. By holding onto the secrets I'd learned, I was doing exactly what the Choir wanted me to do. I was perpetuating the great lie and thus, continuing their work. All while posing as some sort of liberator."

"Mara told me about Raum. And how he broadcast the secret all across Hell," said Anael. "I imagine people aren't very happy about it."

"You'd be surprised," said Lucifer. "Once that initial shock wore off, most simply came to accept it. They all hated the Choir already, so coming to terms with that sort of duplicity from the seraphim was the easy part. It was my role in all this that's spurred the most anger. And that's something I expected, which is why I offered to put myself on trial before the calls for blood began."

"Do you really believe you can get a fair trial in Hell? These are the people who thought you were their savior and now they see you as just a pawn of their oppressors."

Lucifer took a sip of the brandy. "Do I take it you're now willing to accept the truth I once tried to share with you?"

"What, that the Choir invented the concept of the Presence? That it was all a tool for control?" Anael shook her head. "Of course not. I think this entire thing is nonsense."

"Then why are you here?"

Anael stepped up to the table and leaned over it, her azure eyes flashing as she stared into Lucifer's face. "I came here to tell you that I've had it. Stop dragging me into your craziness, Lucifer. It's already cost me more than I'd care to give up."

Lucifer furrowed his brow. "What are you talking about? Cost you what?"

She stood upright. "Uriel's taking credit for getting you to return to Hell, reporting to the Choir that I failed in my assignment because I let my feelings for you interfere with the mission."

"That's ridiculous," said Lucifer. "I haven't *returned* to Hell at all. Cross still sits on the throne. And you tried everything possible to complete your mission, but nothing would force me back onto the throne."

"Uriel only cares about the details that make him look good. And he's now let word spread that I'm compromised. That maybe I'm more loyal to you than Heaven. I haven't dared return to Elysium because of that, so I'm stuck here on Earth."

"All the more reason to help me," said Lucifer. "You take up the cause of defending me, and together we can prove that these structures of control are inhibiting all of us."

"No." Anael crossed her arms. "Listen to me, Lucifer—despite what nonsense Uriel is spreading, I *am* loyal to the Choir and all it stands for. I'm not going to justify Uriel's lies by taking sides with you in some sort of kangaroo court."

"You really believe you'll ever be good enough?" asked Lucifer. "As far as the Choir is concerned, you're forever tainted because of your association with me. Doesn't matter that you were simply trying to do the right thing. Scum like Uriel only deal in absolutes, and they'll twist the truth in whatever shapes are necessary in order to achieve their desires. And the Choir? They don't care at all. As long as they can maintain the status quo, they'll happily swallow whatever Uriel feeds them. They'll sacrifice anyone—even an angel who's been as loyal as you have."

"And if I were to help you, what would that do? How would that benefit me?"

Lucifer looked down. His silence was the clearest answer he could give.

"That's what I thought," said Anael. "There's nothing to be gained from helping you, Lucifer. This is just another war that you'll end up on the losing side of. I refused to fall with you then and I refuse to do it now."

She turned away and her wings emerged from her back. Lucifer called out to her, and his words caused her to wait.

"So what will you do, then?" he asked.

Anael sighed. "I wish I had an answer to that question. All I know is that associating with you has never been anything but disastrous for me."

Rather than using her wings to teleport away, Anael took to the skies. She felt like relishing in the freedom of just flying among the clouds and she didn't give a damn if anyone saw her. All she wanted was freedom from the craziness.

Uriel, Lucifer, all of it. Every time Anael had managed to gain some ground, something happened to set her back. Nothing would ever satisfy either of them. She didn't know how this would end between those two, but she no longer cared, either.

Now that she was a pariah among the angels, she'd have to find a new path.

CHAPTER 2

After Anael had flown off, Lucifer took his drink and walked inside the kitchen. Belial stood at the open refrigerator, scanning the contents. When Lucifer closed the patio door, Belial looked up.

"Don't pretend that you weren't eavesdropping," said Lucifer.

"My apologies," said Belial, closing the refrigerator. "What will you do now that Anael has refused to act in your defense?"

"I knew she would refuse. This is just the first step in the process," said Lucifer. "I'll continue to try to reach her, convince her that this is the right thing to do."

"You heard what she said. You're well aware of how stubborn she can be."

"Yes, she's almost as bad as me, that's something I'm well aware of."

"I never said—"

Lucifer smirked. "You didn't have to. But Anael's tenacity is exactly what I need in that courtroom."

"Why try to seek the defense of someone who has always been antagonistic? Who betrayed you even?" asked Belial. "Why not Mara or myself?"

"Because the problem with either of you is you're *too* loyal. You have more of an emotional investment in this. But Anael, she's different. She doesn't just believe anything I say without evidence to back it up. She's willing to challenge me, and she's capable of seeing what attacks are coming. Whoever the Court appoints to serve as prosecutor is going to be well-informed about my numerous flaws. And Anael has spent eons already thinking of those. Only she'd be able to come up with a defense against them."

Belial leaned back against the refrigerator and slid his hands into his pants pockets. Lucifer watched the demon's eyes fall to the ground and stepped closer towards him.

"You don't agree."

The demon gave a soft huff.

"I thought we were past you being unable to open up to me about these things," said Lucifer. "You can speak freely, Belial."

Belial slowly looked up. "You're making the same mistakes all over again, my lord. How many times have you put your trust in Anael and how many times has she come up short? Even in the time since you've been on Earth, the two of you have been at odds more times than you've been in agreement. She's the one who betrayed you to the Choir before the war."

"And you think I've forgotten that?" asked Lucifer.

"I never said you forgot, I said—"

"You think I'm blind to her actions. What she's done all this time. I promise you, I'm not. Anael and I will never see eye-to-eye, that's something I accepted long ago."

"And yet you continue trying with her. Why?"

"Because of all the celestial beings, none deserve to know the truth of reality more than her. She pledged her life and fealty to the Choir and they've abused that privilege."

"And what makes her more deserving than any other angel? Uriel, Gabriel…Michael?"

Lucifer's face contorted in anger at that name. *Michael.* Before The Fall, Lucifer was regarded as the most beautiful of all the angels, beloved by all. But for Lucifer, there was only one angel he himself admired more than any other—and that was Michael.

First, he had been betrayed by his lover. And then, his idol was the one who came after him, who battled him almost to death. Lucifer could still feel the heat from Michael's soulfire blade as it hovered just over his neck. He instinctively reached a hand for his throat where Michael's blade had almost struck.

"If I'm not mistaken, I believe you have some work to do," said Lucifer. "The sorcerer has requested your presence tonight, hasn't he?"

Lucifer was referring to Odysseus Black, one of the most powerful sorcerers in the country, if not the world. And a key figure in the supernatural underworld. When Lucifer was rendered powerless in his battle against one of the Cocytus escapees, Belial had begun doing odd jobs for Odysseus. It was an arrangement that continued into the present.

"I suppose I do." Yellow light seeped from Belial's back and forged into leathery, demonic wings. "Consider my words, sire. Anael has been nothing but a disappointment at every turn. To put your faith in her is to risk your ultimate freedom."

With that final warning given, Belial wrapped himself in his wings and vanished in a flash of light. Lucifer sighed and raised the brandy glass to his lips to finish off the contents. He picked up the bottle and refilled it when he heard footsteps. Lucifer looked up and saw his two minders standing at the door connecting the kitchen to the library.

"Mr. Moore, it would appear that our dear Morningstar is a bit perturbed, would it not?"

"Indeed it would, Mr. Grant. The Morningstar had hoped this gambit would grant him the freedom he long sought. And yet, is it already unraveling before it's even begun?"

"Don't talk to me," said Lucifer. "You two are only here because Purgatory is neutral in this fight. I've agreed for you to stay in my home, but I never said anything about having to entertain your idiotic two-man routine. So unless you have something of worth to add, I'm not interested in hearing a damn thing you have to say."

Grant and Moore both turned their heads away from Lucifer and inward towards each other. Then they moved in sync and returned their gaze to the Morningstar.

"Neutrality is important, Mr. Grant."

"Quite so, Mr. Moore. And as neutral players in this game—"

"I believe we would technically be classified as 'non-players,' Mr. Grant."

"Ah, right you are, Mr. Moore. As neutral non-players in this game, we are forbidden from interfering in any way."

"And as such, we could not inform Mr. Lucifer of the plots against Ms. Anael, Mr. Grant."

Lucifer set the glass down. "What did you say?"

Grant and Moore once again exchanged glances.

"I don't believe I heard you say anything, Mr. Moore. Am I mistaken in that?"

"Not to my recollection, Mr. Grant. And I certainly

did not hear a word pass your lips, either."

"There's a plot against Anael?" asked Lucifer. "Who is after her?"

Grant and Moore remained silent and just stared off into space. Lucifer considered the possibilities. With Anael no longer welcome in Heaven, it was quite possible that some of the more militant angels could be targeting her, seeing her as a liability to the Choir's will. Or perhaps it was even some of the denizens of Hell. Belial wasn't the only one who had a low opinion of Lucifer's former lover, but he wouldn't act without the Morningstar's permission. There could easily be other demons who would be more recalcitrant.

"What sort of plots are we talking about here?" asked Lucifer. "How do you know all of this?"

"My dear Lucifer, neither Mr. Moore nor myself have acknowledged any sort of insight into any manner of plot against Ms. Anael or any other angel."

"Mr. Grant speaks the truth, Mr. Lucifer. But it is known that Purgatory has eyes and ears everywhere. When one remains neutral, one wishes to know what sort of shenanigans the other sides are getting up to."

"Why must the two of you always speak in riddles? Couldn't Thanatos have created servants that were more direct?"

"It is not our place to interfere, Mr. Lucifer. But if Mr. Grant and I were in your shoes—"

"Mr. Moore is speaking metaphorically, of course. In reality, I doubt we share a size."

"Quite right, Mr. Grant. But if we were in your situation, perhaps we would find the place where Ms. Anael frequents."

When Mara went to deliver the message to Anael, she found the angel in an Uptown bar called The Green Mill. It was a favored spot of Gabriel when he was on Earth and Lucifer had met his brother there on more than one occasion. Lucifer wagered it was Gabriel who introduced Anael to the bar. And it was likely that if Mara could find her there, so could any potential assassins.

"I know where I have to go." Lucifer's feathered wings emerged from his back and before the light could diminish from them, he wrapped them around his body. But just when he was about to teleport from his home, he suddenly found that he couldn't.

Lucifer unfurled the wings and saw Grant and Moore now standing closer to him. "What's happening?"

"Unfortunately, Mr. Grant and I cannot permit you to leave."

"That is unfortunately correct, Mr. Lucifer. Mr. Moore and I are tasked with staying by your side at all times until the trial begins."

"I can't just sit back and do nothing," said Lucifer. "If Anael's life is in danger, I have to go to her."

"Oh, do not get Mr. Grant's words twisted, Mr. Lucifer."

"Apologies if I did not speak plainly, dear Morningstar. But what Mr. Moore is trying to say is that if you need to travel anywhere, then by the terms of the agreement, we must accompany you."

Lucifer groaned. "Fine, but we don't have a car and I certainly can't transport the two of you."

"Quite all right. Mr. Grant and I always come prepared."

"Indeed we do, Mr. Moore."

Grant and Moore turned and faced each other and stepped closer. They clasped their hands together and stepped so that their chests were touching. The two seemed to become one, and when they pulled away from each other, there was a trail of ebon energy that trailed their bodies. It expanded into a full-size doorway through time and space.

"Please allow Mr. Grant and I to act as your transportation."

"Mr. Moore and I would indeed be honored if you would step through our doorway."

The two stood on either side of the portal, each gesturing towards it. Lucifer retracted his wings and stepped up to the dark void. When he peered in, he could see nothing. And he wondered just how this method of transportation worked. But he supposed he had no other choice—he had to be certain Anael was okay.

Lucifer stepped into the void and the mysterious Purgatory agents followed. It closed behind them and they were bathed in the darkness.

CHAPTER 3

I t was a strange experience traveling through whatever void Grant and Moore used for their transportation. Lucifer didn't believe it to be Purgatory—he'd spent time in that realm before and this seemed like something altogether different. It felt even more disconcerting than the first time he'd entered Hell. Colors and shapes moved in a kaleidoscope fashion. He could taste and hear the strange images that engulfed every expanse of this bizarre dimension.

The word "overwhelming" didn't quite do it justice. Lucifer was convinced that if he'd spent any length of time in this bizarre place, he'd be driven completely insane. He wasn't even sure how long he'd been there so far. The moments seemed to flash at a rapid pace while at a same time moving incredibly slow. Yes, this definitely must be what madness felt like.

Cracks formed along the shifting colors and shapes, like they were stained glass just struck by a rock. The cracks spiderwebbed out and one by one, the pieces fell into nothingness, giving way back to the real world.

Lucifer was suddenly standing in the intersection between Lawrence and Broadway. The blaring of car horns drew his attention to the present. A car swerved to avoid him, nearly striking another in the outside lane. But another driver didn't seem as capable of dodging the retired King of Hell.

Now fully alert, Lucifer jumped onto the hood of the car, much to the driver's shock. The car skidded to a stop, swerving to the side, the sound of rubber squealing across the pavement. The blare of another car horn and Lucifer saw a truck barreling on them. He jumped off the hood and held out his hands. Waves of distortion appeared in the air as he used his powers to slow the momentum of the truck, long enough for the driver he'd just surprised to regain his faculties and drive off. Lucifer stepped onto the curb and released his hold on the truck, allowing order to be restored.

"Very impressive work, don't you think, Mr. Grant?"

"Quite impressive, Mr. Moore. Our Mr. Morningstar seems to have withstood his trials and come out it the other end."

Lucifer glared at the two suited agents of Purgatory that suddenly stood in front of him. "You couldn't have dropped me off in an alley or at the very least a sidewalk?"

Grant and Moore exchanged glances hidden behind their sunglasses, then turned their heads in unison back towards Lucifer. They offered no further words. Lucifer waved a dismissive hand and walked past the pair. Just ahead of him, located on the corner of Broadway and Lawrence, was The Green Mill. He entered the jazz club and as soon as he passed through the doors, the sounds of brass instruments filled the air.

Lucifer moved through the bar, sensing Anael's presence in here. He didn't even need his eyes, an angel stood out to one with his sensory perception like a spotlight in a pitch-dark room. He walked passed the tables until he found a booth where she sat on her own, nursing a gin and tonic. Her eyes were directed at the musicians onstage, but she wasn't really paying attention to them.

Before he approached her, he stopped and just watched her. The way she brushed strands of her long, raven hair behind her ear, how her fingers toyed with the straw in her drink, the curve of her elegant neck. His memories flashed back to memories of Elysium, before The Fall. When the two of them shared a bond unlike anything he'd ever experienced before or since.

Those days were long over and it seemed impossible to ever gain even a semblance of them back. Regardless of the past, Lucifer still felt responsible for Anael. If she was indeed in danger, he had to do everything in his power to protect her.

He realized then that he'd been staring at her. But worse, she'd noticed and now met his gaze with a steely one of her own. She scoffed and turned away, about to rise from her booth. Lucifer moved quick and slid into the booth across from her.

"What's the rush?" he asked.

"We've already said all there is to say. No need to drag things out any further." She shot him a glare. "I've already told you, my answer's no."

Lucifer gently held her back by her shoulder. "I'm not here about that."

"Then what?" she asked. "What in Heaven's name do you want from me now?"

"This isn't about me—"

Her chortle interrupted him. "Really? I thought everything was?"

Lucifer sighed audibly. One thing Anael could do better than anyone else was rile him up. "Could you please just listen for ten seconds?"

"Fine." She leaned back against the booth's cushion and crossed her arms. "Ten…nine…"

"Do you have to be so childish?"

"Seven…six…five…"

"Your life is in danger, Ana. There are forces coming for you and now that you're not under Heaven's protection, you're vulnerable to att—"

"Two…one…and that's time." She slid out of the booth and stood. "Do me a favor, Morningstar—sell your snake oil to someone dumb enough to swallow it. Because I've had it with you."

Lucifer sighed and lowered his head into his hands.

"T'would seem there's some trouble in paradise, Mr. Moore."

"So it t'would, Mr. Grant. So it t'would."

He lifted his head and groaned when he saw the two Purgatory agents seated across from him where Anael had just been. "Do you mind?"

"Mind? Mr. Grant has no mind to mind."

"Nor, in point of fact, does Mr. Moore."

"That's becoming painfully and annoyingly clear." Lucifer climbed out of the booth and went after Anael. She had already reached the front door and had stepped outside by the time he reached her.

"Ana, could you please just listen to me?"

"Why would I bother?" she asked. "You're nothing but a pain in my ass and your attempt to make up some story about my life being threatened is just ridiculously transparent."

"I didn't make anything up. The Purgatory agents told me about it."

She stopped and turned on her heel. "Oh, so the cryptic nightmare twins tell you something and you just believe it?"

"What reason would they have to lie?" asked Lucifer.

She shrugged. "Who knows what Thanatos is up to? He's as old as Death and the Presence, predating Heaven itself. I can't pretend to understand his motivations, but I'm certain that there's nothing good about them."

"If you would only wait and try to figure this out. You have no one else to back you up should anything happen."

Anael's eyes glanced to the ground and she hesitated before saying, "Come with me." She turned around and walked ahead to the entrance of the Lawrence subway station, then descended the stairs.

Lucifer stopped at the foot of the stairs and looked down at her. She stopped and looked back at him, her eyes casting a soft, blue glow on the darkened staircase.

"Are you coming or what?"

He was skeptical of what she wanted, but at least this way he could keep an eye on her. Lucifer jogged down the steps to catch up to her. They moved onto the train platform and at this time of night, there was no one around.

Anael grabbed Lucifer and slammed him against the wall. There was a burst of blue flame and suddenly, a soulfire blade was clutched in her hand and placed at the edge of his throat. Lucifer kept his head back, trying to put as much distance between the blade and his neck as possible. Anael stared at him with her fierce, blue eyes.

"You see how easily I turned the tables on you?" she asked. "Even if it were true, even if there is someone out there to get me, I think I've proved by this point that I'm *more* than capable of defending myself."

"You'll certainly get no argument from me on that front. But it wouldn't hurt to have someone watching your back," said Lucifer.

"You're right, but it wouldn't be you, Adversary." The soulfire blade dissolved into the air and she drove her elbow into Lucifer's face, slamming his head against the wall. She turned away from him. "I'd never trust a traitor to look out for me."

"Is that still the way you see it, after all this time?"

Anael glanced over her shoulder. "Is there any other way?"

"Let's remember which of us *actually* betrayed the other," said Lucifer. "Or have you forgotten how I ended up imprisoned in Gehenna?"

"That was different. I was trying to stop you from making the greatest mistake of your life. Had you just fallen in line, you would have eventually been released and we'd still be together."

"And all it would have cost me was my soul," said Lucifer. "I wasn't prepared to perpetuate a lie just so the Choir could maintain their chokehold on Heaven."

"You see?" asked Anael, turning to him. "There really *is* nothing more to say. We just keep running around in these same circles. The same arguments, perpetually going back and forth."

"That's why I'm trying to break the cycle."

"You can't." Anael's wings emerged from her back and they wrapped around her lithe body. "Goodbye, Morningstar. I hope this trial finally gives you what you deserve."

Before Anael could transport herself away, a chain came out of nowhere and wrapped itself around her neck. Anael struggled to pull free, but other chains suddenly appeared from the darkness, wrapping around each of her limbs and wings, pulling them all taut and stretching her out.

"What's happening?" she demanded.

Lucifer generated twin hellfire swords in his hands and his wings emerged from his back. "Do you believe me now?"

"You can gloat all you want once you get me out of these things!" she demanded.

Lucifer's hellfire swords quickly made short work of Anael's restraints, freeing her from their confines. But soon, more came from the darkness, wrapping around the both of them. Lucifer and Anael both tried to sever as many of the links as possible, but there seemed no limit to their number. They quickly felt themselves becoming exhausted and soon, they were restrained once more.

Heavy footfalls echoed in the subway tunnels, accompanied by the rattle of what seemed like dozens of chains. A figure emerged from the darkness, wrapped completely in leather. Only his azure eyes were visible, and they burned in the black. He climbed onto the platform and approached his new prisoners, examining the two of them closely.

"Anael, you poor thing. You've fallen so far because of the Adversary's machinations." His voice had a high pitch to it, a sharp contrast from his brutish, tank-like form.

"I don't know what you've been told, but—"

"Silence!" The mysterious hulk waved his hand and chains wrapped around Anael's jaw, preventing her from speaking. His attention next fell on Lucifer. "And you.

It's been eons since I last saw you, Morningstar. Do you remember the time we once spent together when you were my ward in Gehenna? I was ever so sad when you left."

"Of course I remember, Kushiel," said Lucifer. "How could I ever forget the one being in all creation who had tortured me?"

Kushiel smiled through the mouth opening in his mask. He reached a hand for Lucifer's face and gripped his chin tightly. "We'll be reunited soon, my pet. And oh, what fun we'll have!"

"What are you doing here, Kushiel?" asked Lucifer. "Since when do you *ever* leave Gehenna?"

"Since the Divine Choir granted my request," said Kushiel. "You see, Lucifer, they're done playing games with you. And I was only too happy to accept their generous offer. Nothing in all the glory of the Presence would give me greater joy than the power to inflict the most righteous of unimaginable tortures upon you. Both you…" he turned Lucifer's head in Anael's direction, "…and your whore!"

CHAPTER 4

As ludicrous as it may have sounded, Heaven had a prison of its own—a desolate structure known as Gehenna where the inmates were kept in solitary confinement. It was designed for angels, so their cells had clear ceilings. The purpose was to force them to always look up to the sky, but be kept from it. The only contact they had with any other beings was the prison's warden—the angel Kushiel.

When Lucifer first began his rule in Hell, he didn't want prisons of any kind, but it soon became a necessity. He had recalled his own time in Gehenna with vivid clarity and sought to make Cocytus a more humane institution. The inmates, of course, didn't see it that way.

But now Kushiel was on Earth—a trip he had never made in his entire life. And both Lucifer and Anael were at his mercy. Soulfire allowed angels to generate almost any tool or weapon they could imagine. Kushiel's almost without fail took the form of chains.

"Soon, we'll all be together again," said Kushiel, gently stroking Lucifer's cheek.

The angel's very touch made Lucifer's skin crawl and his mind continued flashing back to the torment he suffered at this creature's hands. The irony was that this *angel* was more of a demon than anything Hell had ever touched. All angels were trained to be relentless warriors. But Kushiel was a sadist of the highest order. If he were to take them to Gehenna, Lucifer didn't even want to think of what terrors would be inflicted upon them.

"Kushiel, maybe we could talk first," said Lucifer.

Through the opening in his leather mask, Kushiel's lips curved downwards. He wrapped his meaty fingers around Lucifer's neck and began to squeeze. "What need is there for talk, Morningstar? You're my prisoner now and you'll do as *I* command, not the other way around."

"No one…disputes that…" Lucifer struggled to say. "You'd at least…permit me some speech before we go?"

"Parting words for this damnable mudball?" Kushiel seemed to contemplate the request for several moments and then released his hold. He took a step back and folded his arms over his broad chest—bare except for the twin leather straps that crossed from his belt to over his shoulders.

"Look at you, Kushiel. So magnificent. You are truly unique among all the angels," said Lucifer.

"What are you doing?" Anael called out in a hushed voice, her words strained due to her own restraints.

"Shut up!" Lucifer snapped back in a similarly hushed tone. He then continued to address Kushiel. "How many prisoners does Heaven really have?"

Kushiel gave a grunt in response.

"Not many, that's what I thought," said Lucifer. "The Choir considers Gehenna to be a deterrent. Like a nuclear bomb—always there, but never intended for actual use. In fact, since The Fall, I'd wager you could count the number of inmates who have been under your care on one hand. Am I wrong?"

"Whatever point you're trying to make, get to it fast," said Kushiel.

"Your life is about punishment, Kushiel. The human souls that reside in Heaven, they're kept in their own little worlds, segregated from each other and certainly from the angels. And angels are a very obedient bunch, so transgressions are rare, correct?"

Lucifer paused and waited for Kushiel to give some sort of a response. The jailer narrowed his eyes through the slits in the mask and said in a drawn-out manner, "Correct."

"Precisely my point. Your gifts—your *talents*—they're being wasted in Heaven. But think of Hell."

"Lucifer, no!" Anael cautioned.

Kushiel stepped closer, his arms slowly lowering to his sides. "What about Hell?"

"It's a place of demons. Imagine all the souls down there in dire need of punishment," said Lucifer.

"Hell has its own torturers."

"Who, Beelzebub?" Lucifer scoffed. "Do you really consider a *grigori* capable of elevating torture to the artform that you have?"

Kushiel grunted. "Of course not. The grigori are nothing more than sad, pathetic voyeurs."

"Now imagine if we had someone like you down there," said Lucifer. "Someone who could show them what torture *truly* means."

"Are you...suggesting I resign my post in Heaven?" asked Kushiel.

"Only because I truly believe your talents would be better served elsewhere. In a place where you have no rules and you can indulge yourself," said Lucifer.

There was a tug at the corner of Kushiel's lips and for a moment, Lucifer thought he'd managed to convince the angel. But it wouldn't last. Kushiel quickly backhanded Lucifer with the force of a meteor. If not for the chains, Lucifer would have been thrown into the far wall—perhaps even *through* it.

"You think me so feeble-minded as to fall for your silver-tongued chicanery?" asked Kushiel.

"Can't blame a fellow for trying…" muttered Lucifer.

"I'm no fool, Morningstar. I understand and accept my place in the celestial order. I'm not so arrogant and prideful to believe myself exempt from the rules that govern this universe. But perhaps you need a lesson *before* we return to Gehenna."

Kushiel's eyes emitted an intense glow and soulfire co-alesced in his open palms. He held out his hand and as his fingers moved, Lucifer felt the chains shifting around his body. One chain wrapped around his neck and tightened. And from the center sprouted two forked prongs, one end bracing itself against Lucifer's sternum and the other pushing under his jaw.

"The Heretic's Fork," said Kushiel. "A fitting accessory for a blasphemer such as yourself."

Lucifer struggled to try and speak, but he couldn't. The fork prevented him from moving his jaw in even as limited a manner as Anael had been capable of moments earlier.

Kushiel turned from Lucifer and moved over to Anael. The chains around her body and her head loosened at his gesture. "You, however, have an opportunity. The Choir has a proposition for you. A chance to renounce the Devil and once more be welcomed into the gates of Elysium."

"And just like that, all is forgiven?" asked Anael.

"Not quite," said Kushiel. "You will need to make restitution for your failure to fulfill your duties."

"What sort of restitution?" asked Anael.

"You must prove your fealty to the Choir. Demonstrate that you truly care nothing for this traitor."

"And how exactly would I go about that?" asked Anael.

Kushiel's smile widened. "Become my apprentice."

Anael's eyes widened in horror. "I beg your pardon?"

"Join me in torturing your former lover. Once the Choir believes you have sufficiently proved your loyalty, you will be allowed to return to Elysium. And never again will you have to set foot upon the desolation that is the Earth."

Anael turned her head from Kushiel and looked upon Lucifer. The Morningstar wondered just what sort of thoughts were running through her head. Did she so despise him now that she'd be willing to accept whatever scraps the Choir threw at her? Was she so desperate to be welcomed back by the very people who'd shunned her?

"And if I refuse?" she asked.

"One way or another, you *will* go to Gehenna," said Kushiel. "The question is will it be as inmate or guard?"

Anael closed her eyes and took a deep breath, apparently thinking over the offer. The anticipation sent Lucifer's stomach falling into a pit while Kushiel couldn't help the smile upon his lips.

"Thank you, Kushiel," she said before opening her eyes. "But I'd rather be tortured than sacrifice my integrity."

Lucifer would have laughed if he could. Kushiel was driven into a rage by her response and the chains around her spouted barbs and tightened. The metal spires pricked

Anael's flesh and now Lucifer struggled against his bonds. He was content to stall for as long as possible, but now he had to move fast.

The Morningstar's entire body burned with an intense, yellow light. Kushiel's attention was drawn from Anael to Lucifer like a moth to flame. The heat Lucifer's power generated could be felt even by those walking above-ground and light poured out from the entrance to the subway.

The Heretic's Fork bent under the heat and became useless. The chains that held the Morningstar melted to slag. He yanked the Heretic's Fork from his neck and incinerated it in his palm. And before Kushiel could process what was happening, Lucifer directed all that energy in his body into his hands, unleashing a powerful burst of hellfire that sent Heaven's jailer flying into the subway tunnel.

With Kushiel's concentration broken, the chains around Anael dissipated in a puff of blue smoke. Lucifer looked down at her, the hellfire still burning in his eyes.

"How do you feel?"

Anael placed her palms together and as she drew them apart, a trail of soulfire followed until she held a heavy broadsword in her hand. "Like killing something."

"Good, because he's coming back," said Lucifer. "And I spent a lot of energy with that display just now."

"You need to learn to pace yourself, Luc," she said.

"I know, I—" Lucifer did a double-take. "Wait, did you just call me—"

"Here he comes!" said Anael.

Kushiel lumbered from the tunnel and jumped onto the platform. He crouched and slammed his fists on the ground. Ripples of soulfire extended out in a shockwave, forging into tentacle-like chains that were tipped with razor-sharp blades.

Lucifer summoned twin swords in his hands and looked at Anael's larger weapon. "You might want something with a bit more speed and maneuverability."

"Are you telling me what to do?" she asked.

"Just a suggestion."

"I can take care of myself, thank you."

"Suit yourself."

Lucifer went into action, cutting through the chains as they came at him. They seemed to be everywhere at once and he was having trouble keeping up with all of them. He chanced a look at Anael and saw that she had indeed changed to twin blades as well. Too stubborn to admit he was right. He couldn't help but smile at that bit of knowledge.

But the fight wouldn't last long. In fact, it had barely started when a swirling, black vortex suddenly separated Kushiel from his targets. Ink-black sludge rose from the vortex, quickly shaping itself into two distinct silhouettes—two that had become quite familiar to Lucifer in recent days.

"My, my, what a mess we have here, Mr. Grant."

"I daresay the Chicago Transit Authority will *not* be pleased, Mr. Moore."

"The poor devils *do* have their work cut out for them, Mr. Grant."

"And speaking of 'poor devils,' Mr. Moore. Just look at what sort of scene we have chanced upon."

"What is the meaning of this?" demanded Kushiel.

Grant and Moore both clasped their hands behind their backs and approached the angel. They bowed in unison before him and then each knelt down on the opposite knee—Grant on his left, Moore on his right.

"We must say it is quite an honor to make your acquaintance, Mr. Kushiel."

"Indeed so. You have long-been an inspiration to us both."

Kushiel scoffed. "So Lucifer chose to summon some demon underlings as opposed to fighting his own battles."

"Did you hear that, Mr. Moore? Our new friend believes us to be servants of the Morningstar."

"And here I thought my ears were mistaken, Mr. Grant, but you are correct. Such an absurd notion."

"If you're not of Hell, then…?"

"Mr. Grant and I are servants of neither Heaven nor Hell."

"My associate, Mr. Moore and myself, instead are agents of the personification of the third realm. Perhaps you have heard of it, Mr. Kushiel?"

Kushiel grunted and the chains began dissipating. "Purgatory. What possible interest could Thanatos have in this matter?"

"The Morningstar over there is soon to be put on trial before the citizenry of Hell, Mr. Kushiel."

"And as a condition of his release, our master has agreed to serve as a neutral arbiter. Mr. Moore and I have been tasked with keeping watch over the defendant until such a time as the trial can begin."

"Mr. Grant speaks nothing but the truth, Mr. Kushiel. We have been ordered to ensure that the Morningstar is not only monitored, but also kept alive until such time as his trial concludes."

"If the Divine Choir chooses to intervene in this matter, then Purgatory will have no choice but to cease being a neutral third-party."

"And we find it highly suspect that the Divine Choir would want to see an alliance between Hell and Purgatory."

"The enemy of mine enemy and all that, you see."

Lucifer and Anael approached the trio as Grant and Moore rose back up to their feet.

"The choice is yours, Kushiel. Do you think the Choir is interested in making a new enemy today?" asked Lucifer.

Kushiel growled as his eyes darted between the four. "Do not think that the Choir won't hear of this."

"I'm counting on it," said Lucifer.

Massive wings emerged from Kushiel's back, bound in leather straps. They wrapped around his body and he vanished in a flash of azure light. Once he was gone, Anael looked at Lucifer.

"You knew, didn't you? That those two would come after you?"

"Simply stalling for time," said Lucifer. "I knew they wouldn't let anything happen to me before the trial."

"That is highly offensive, Mr. Lucifer. Do not think of Mr. Grant and I as your bodyguards."

"Though Mr. Moore and myself are tasked with keeping you safe, any indignities we suffer as a result of our services will be remembered by our master."

"It wasn't my intention to presume on our relationship. I hadn't expected Kushiel of all people to come after me," said Lucifer.

"This does indeed pose a conundrum, eh Mr. Moore?"

"I would be forced to concur, Mr. Grant."

Lucifer turned his attention back to Anael. "So you've

seen what Heaven now thinks of you. What will you do now?"

Anael shook her head. "Nothing's changed, Lucifer. I'm still not interested in defending you in this ridiculous trial. Doesn't matter how many sycophants Heaven throws my way."

Her wings unfurled and within moments, she wrapped herself in them and was gone. That left Lucifer standing alone in the subway with his two minders.

"All things considered, I'd say that went about as well as could be expected," he said.

CHAPTER 5

There were eight major territories in Hell, separated by vast distances of unclaimed stretches known simply as the Badlands. Each of the territories was governed by one of the Infernal Court. Initially, there had been nine. But after Abraxas's attempted coup, his territory was divided amongst the other Hell Lords.

The territories themselves reflected the nature of their stewards. The area controlled by the Hell Lord Mammon was bordered by walls of solid gold. While most of the Hell Lords had castles built for their homes, Mammon's was instead a giant, gold tower in the middle of the kingdom. At the top of the tower were characters from the Dimoori Sheol—the demonic language of Hell—that spelled out his name.

From his penthouse home, Mammon looked down on his lands. He wore a dark blue suit with red tie and his light-colored hair was swept in a pile on his head. He turned his attention to the two guests who had recently arrived in secret. The other two Hell Lords sat at a long table on opposite sides.

Beelzebub appeared as a giant insect. While the other demons possessed leathery wings, his had more in common with the gossamer appendages that fit his title as Lord of the Flies.

Leviathan was the other and similarly transformed, although in a different way. She was a serpentine-like creature with brownish-green scales all over her body and a pronounced snout and mouth.

The purpose of this gathering was to discuss the impending trial. Beelzebub had already betrayed Lucifer, attempting to eliminate the former King of Hell through the use of a demon named Raum. That plot failed, but the one silver lining was it had opened up this opportunity.

"So the three of us are in agreement," said Mammon. "No matter what and no matter how, Lucifer must pay for his crimes."

"We trusssted him, and all thisss time he was still keeping the Choir's secrets," said Leviathan.

"My own feelings should be clear," said Beelzebub. "Hizzz abdication convinced me he was no longer fit. But after what Raum uncovered…"

Before The Fall, the Divine Choir had indoctrinated angels into believing in the existence of some benevolent, omniscient higher power—what they referred to as the Presence. Lord of all the universe and the one they must dedicate their lives to the service of. When Lucifer learned the truth, he launched a rebellion. But while he championed the cause of free will, he never told any of his followers that the Presence was a lie. Even after The Fall, he maintained that secret, only recently passing on the information to his successor, Luther Cross.

Once Raum revealed the truth, it sent shockwaves reverberating throughout Hell. And that was the reason for Lucifer to put himself on trial.

"Lucifer was an absentee landlord at best. After the initial setbacks, his only goal was maintaining the tenuous peace with Heaven," said Mammon. "Think of how many of our own kind he imprisoned in Cocytus just to appease the Choir."

"So much for rebelling," said Beelzebub. "He never stopped serving!"

"But there's a problem," said Leviathan. "Despite the Morningstar's failures, the cult of personality remainsss sstrong, even now. So many willing to simply forgive and forget. Even among the Court itself. Only we three are firmly in favor of punishment."

"Cross is of course in favor of acquittal," said Mammon. "As is Lilith."

"Why would she be for acquittal?" asked Beelzebub. "She wazzz one of the first victims of Cocytus, thrown in there for the Choir's benefit."

"It's baffling to me as well, but that's the situation," said Mammon. "I understand that Vassago also supports acquittal."

"That's no surprise," said Leviathan. "He was always a spinelessss yes-man, willing to follow whomever is in charge. At the moment, that jussst so happens to be Cross."

"What of Nergal and Abaddon? You've said nothing of them," said Beelzebub.

Mammon shrugged. "They've remained neutral thus far. No desire to take a position one way or the other. We'll see how long that lasts, though."

"If the people were to decide today, they would acquit. Such izz Lucifer's hold over their hearts and minds," said Beelzebub.

"Unfortunately true." Mammon approached the table

and sat at the head. He rested his elbows on the surface and interlocked his fingers. "So how do we undo eons of propaganda?"

"Ssshow his victims," said Leviathan. "We need a prosecutor who is every bit as charming and intelligent as the Morningstar. Someone who could truly stand up to him and convince Hell of his guilt."

"That leaves out the three of us," said Beelzebub.

"What makes you say that?" asked Mammon.

Beelzebub turned his head and stared at Mammon with giant, insectoid eyes. "Do I *really* need to explain why? All you have to do is *look* at Leviathan and myself. And azz for you, you sit here in a tower while your people beg for scraps. No Hell Lord is considered more corrupt and selfish than you."

"I can't say I care much for that characterization." Mammon frowned and leaned back in his chair. "I mean, it's a fair one. But hurts to hear out loud."

"In retrossspect, Raum would have been perfect," said Leviathan. "A champion of the people, ssstanding up to tyranny. That would have made for a brilliant narrative— Lucifer as the puppet, Raum as the true revolutionary."

"Yeah, well he's been atomized. So please try to focus on *actual* possibilities over would-haves, could-haves, should-haves," said Mammon.

"What about the demon Raum learned it all from?" asked Beelzebub.

Mammon and Leviathan both turned their attention to the Lord of the Flies. Beelzebub met their gazes, his mouth twitching.

"Raum's mentor wazzz also a victim of Cocytus," said Beelzebub. "And since the prison's been demolished, he's wandering the Badlands somewhere. No doubt interested in revenge against not only the Morningstar, but Luther Cross azz well."

"You don't mean…?"

Beelzebub nodded.

"Could he even be trusted?" asked Mammon.

"Doezzz it matter?" asked Beelzebub. "We only need him to get a conviction. We can deal with the consequences later."

"The Court will have to agree on any appointment and Cross and Lilith are liable to vote no," said Leviathan.

"All we need is a simple majority," said Beelzebub. "If we could convince Nergal and Abaddon, we'd succeed."

"I'll ssspeak with Nergal," said Leviathan. "He's a fellow warrior and we fought many battles side-by-side."

"I can speak to Abaddon then," said Mammon. "But all of this is moot if our old friend refuses to accept this role. What do you think, Beelzebub? Can you find him *and* get him to agree?"

"Oh yes, I think that will be the eazzy part," said Beelzebub with a smile. "Trust me, he'll do whatever it takes for vengeance on his enemies."

CHAPTER 6

Eden served as a kind of embassy for the Divine Choir. It was located in a small pocket dimension between Heaven and Earth, and it had been constructed in the form of a piano bar. The current caretaker was the angel Uriel, and if he had his way, he would have chosen a different kind of decor. He didn't care for this sort of atmosphere. But a predecessor had and those that frequented seemed to like it that way. So Uriel was content to let it stand in its current form.

At the moment, he stood on the club's large balcony. Just over the edge was the swirling void between dimensions, colors moving together in intricate patterns. Uriel felt good, for probably the first time since he'd been assigned to this post. He never wanted anything to do with Earth in the first place and the task he'd been given by the Choir seemed impossible—get the Morningstar back in Hell where he belonged.

If there was one thing Uriel had learned in his long life, it was the importance of delegation. And so he gave the task to the one angel he thought had the best chance of convincing Lucifer to change his mind. It didn't work, of course. Anael had proven to be a failure of judgment.

But Lucifer's fortuitous loss of powers gave Uriel just the situation he needed. He'd sent bumbling assassins after the Morningstar, confident they would fail, but also that a brush with certain death would convince Lucifer to try and reclaim his powers in Hell.

It had worked. Lucifer returned to the pit and as an added bonus, Uriel was able to expel the insubordinate Anael from Eden. Things had been quiet ever since, and he was enjoying the calm.

But of course, the calm only preceded the storm. And the first signal of the storm came from the presence of one of Uriel's staff. He could sense her stepping out onto the balcony without even turning. Uriel finished off his wine and set the glass down.

"Naomi, I assume there's a reason you're just standing there in silence," he said.

The angel hesitated before she spoke and her voice halted in a few key places. Almost struggling to get the words out. "I apologize for disturbing you, but there's been a...a development....of sorts..."

Uriel turned and looked at the red-haired angel. Her head was bowed and her eyes closed, while her posture with her shuffling hands conveyed a certain anxious quality.

"What 'development' would that be, my dear?" asked Uriel.

"As per your orders, we've had some informants keep tabs on Anael. Most of her nights have been spent at some bar in Chicago. But one development was an appearance by one of Lilith's demons, the one called Mara. And the other—"

"And what business did the manager of Lust have with our little exile? A job offer, perhaps?" Uriel chuckled at the image of Anael bartending at a club full of demons.

"The truth is we're not sure. Our informant couldn't get close enough to hear what they discussed, and it was a short conversation," said Naomi. "At first, we didn't think it of any import."

Uriel cocked a brow. "I beg your pardon?"

"It was…a report of no significance," said Naomi. "Nothing of substance to mention."

"Let me see if I've properly grasped the situation." Uriel crossed the distance over to Naomi and placed his hands on her shoulders. "One of Hell's emissaries on Earth took a meeting with an exiled angel who also just so happens to be the Morningstar's former lover…and you *didn't* think it was of any significance?"

"I…apologize, Uriel."

Uriel raised his hand to Naomi's scarlet hair and began stroking it, his fingers playing through the red strands. "Naomi, remind me what your mission is."

"I have been assigned to Eden to serve at your behest."

"Exactly."

Uriel's gentle strokes came to an abrupt end when he grabbed a fistful of Naomi's hair and pulled it hard, yanking her head back. She yelped at the sudden jolt of pain on her head.

He brought his face in close to her ear and hissed his next words. "So when I tell you I want to know *every damn move* made by that seditious bitch, *it's not a matter of fucking interpretation!*"

He shoved her away and Naomi struck the balcony railing, almost toppling over the edge. She steadied herself and got down on her knees. "I beg your forgiveness, my lord! I wasn't thinking and—"

"No, actually, you *were* thinking. And that's the problem," said Uriel. "You're not here to think, wench. You're here to do as you're told. Is that understood, or do I have to draw it in crayon for you?"

Naomi shook her head and bowed lower, resting her head atop her splayed hands. "No, sir. I now see the error of my ways, and thank you for educating me."

"Good. Now get on your feet," said Uriel.

Naomi rose up and when she stood straight, she still kept her head bowed and her hands clasped together.

"Now, you spoke of more than one development," said Uriel. "What was the other?"

"It's...well, you aren't going to like it, sir."

Uriel's nostrils flared in response. "Did I ask for you to editorialize?"

Naomi's shoulders stiffened and she shook her head. "No, sir."

"Then spit it out already!"

"It's...Anael was spotted again at that very same bar. With the Morningstar."

Uriel's lips tightened. "Lucifer is back on Earth? Since when?"

Naomi shook her head. "Forgive me, sir, but I don't have that information. Unfortunately, that is not the most dire piece of news. Our informant followed them when they left the bar. They apparently went into a subway where they were attacked."

Uriel chuckled at that. "Well, now we're talking!" He gave Naomi an exuberant slap on her back. But when he noticed her expression hadn't changed, his own excitement quickly turned to concern. "Why aren't you happy about this?"

"Sir, apparently they were attacked by an angel."

Uriel's eyes narrowed. "Which angel?"

Naomi looked up at him for a brief instant and opened her mouth. But she quickly averted her eyes before she spoke the name in a barely audible voice. "Kushiel, sir."

Uriel felt more confused by that revelation than anything else. "You're certain?"

"Based on the description the informant gave, it could *only* have been Kushiel, sir."

Kushiel would have never come to Earth of his own volition. He was a loyal subject, always willing to do the bidding of the Divine Choir. The only way he would ever come to Earth would be if he was ordered to do so. And that left the question of why the Choir would dispatch Heaven's jailer without first speaking with Uriel. After all, this was his sphere of influence and he specifically was tasked with the Lucifer problem.

"Sir...?" asked Naomi, her tone cautious.

Uriel realized he'd been lost in his own thoughts. "Thank you, Naomi. I appreciate you bringing this matter to my attention. Now if you'll excuse me, there's something I have to do."

Normally, angels unfurling their wings was frowned upon in Eden. But at the moment, Uriel didn't care. His wings emerged from his back and carried him up several levels above Eden's base floor. None had access to this uppermost level other than Uriel himself. He needed an audience with the Divine Choir, to discover what was going on.

Uriel stepped onto the private balcony and walked inside the empty, white room. He held his hand out and his blue eyes shimmered as soulfire manifested at the tips of his fingers. An Enochian sigil formed on the ground in response to his hand movements and once he had completed the work, he knelt down in the center of the marking. Uriel's back was straight and his hands rested on his thighs while he closed his eyes and began chanting a prayer in Enochian.

Energy seeped out from the sigil and the projection of a figure began to appear in front of him. It was another angel, this one with a bald head and dark skin. Uriel was somewhat irritated to see which angel had answered his summons. He had hoped for Michael, but instead it was Gabriel that he now had to go through to reach the Divine Choir.

"Hello, Uriel," said Gabriel. "You rang?"

"Where's Michael? I need to speak with him," said Uriel.

"Michael is otherwise occupied at the moment and you know full-well that mine is the role of messenger," said Gabriel.

"In this situation, you also have a conflict of interest."

Gabriel didn't react to Uriel's provocations. "What do you want, emissary?"

"I want to know why my authority is being undermined," said Uriel.

"I'm sure I have no idea what you're babbling about."

"Lucifer, you simpleton. The Divine Choir tasked me with dealing with him."

"Your point?" asked Gabriel.

"Why have I received reports that Lucifer and Anael were attacked by Kushiel of all people?"

"I don't know what you're talking about," said Gabriel.

Uriel studied the angel's face. When he'd mentioned

Kushiel, Gabriel visibly stiffened. He clearly knew something, but wasn't providing any details.

"You're lying."

Gabriel sighed. "Uriel, you were given this post because the Choir felt you were someone who could deliver results and remain impartial in the process. But I'm sensing a high degree of emotion coming from you. No doubt the Choir is aware of this as well, and of how it would negatively impact your ability to remain a neutral arbiter."

"You're a fine one to talk. As I recall, it was your own affinity for the talking monkeys that run around this planet that caused the Choir to restrict you to Heaven."

"This isn't about me, is it?" asked Gabriel. "For the sake of argument, let's say that the Choir *has* dispatched Kushiel after the Morningstar. If I were in your position, that would be a signal to me that I should be worried about how the Choir is evaluating my performance. Going around one's back would suggest a lack of confidence in one's ability to properly do their job. Wouldn't you agree?"

Uriel had to restrain his anger. The Choir was playing games with him and he didn't appreciate it. After doing everything they'd asked of him, now they tossed him aside the second there was a hiccup in his performance. It certainly wasn't his fault that Anael failed so spectacularly in her assigned task. And he *had* managed to get Lucifer back to Hell…even if it apparently was only temporary.

"Tell Michael I need an audience with him immediately. He's the general of Heaven's armies and Lucifer's return to Earth could mark a resumption of hostilities," said Uriel. "This is now a military matter."

"We both know that's a load of crap," said Gabriel.

"I didn't ask for your opinion," said Uriel. "You're

Heaven's messenger, Gabriel. So deliver the damn message. Or I'll find some other way to get word to Michael. And you probably won't like my methods."

"Sounds like a threat to me, Uriel."

"I don't threaten—I promise."

Uriel's eyes flashed and the sigil he knelt on vanished. With that, the connection to Heaven was severed and Gabriel's image vanished.

Lucifer back from Hell and Kushiel on his trail. Something was happening, and Uriel would have to discover what. And apparently, he would have to learn the truth without any assistance from the Choir. That meant some more unconventional means were necessary.

Uriel left his private space and returned to the balcony attached to Eden. He called out for Naomi and she appeared just a moment later, meeting him just as his feet touched down.

"Yes, sir?" she asked.

"Start making overtures to the demon community. I want someone to tell me what exactly is happening in Hell and how it involves Lucifer."

"You want me to speak to demons…?" asked Naomi.

"Indirectly and discretely," said Uriel. "Something is brewing and I need to know what."

CHAPTER 7

Anael was perched at the top of the John Hancock Tower. The attack by Kushiel played on a loop in her head. All she wanted was to finally be free of this madness, but it seemed that wish was out of reach.

"Penny for 'em?"

The voice gave her a start. She wasn't expecting any company all the way up here, and so she wasn't even paying attention to her celestial senses. Anael quickly recovered and glanced over her shoulder to see the angel Gabriel hovering just behind her, wearing a soft smile on his lips.

"Something tells me we shouldn't be speaking," said Anael.

Gabriel flew around and came to a hover right in front of her. "I was hoping I'd find you at The Green Mill. It's been too long since I was there."

"Too many people have turned up there since I started going. Felt I needed to just be away from everyone." Anael met his gaze. "What are you doing here, Gabriel? The stick didn't work, so now you're going to try the carrot?"

"I understand why you'd say that," he said. "But I didn't know about Kushiel. I only just learned of it myself, and it was Uriel who told me."

"And how did he find out?" asked Anael.

"He's had people following you. You should be more careful."

"Hence why I'm up here."

"Touché."

"Why did the Choir send Kushiel after me?" asked Anael. "I did what I was told. I can't be held responsible for Lucifer's stubbornness."

"I wish I knew," said Gabriel, moving to her side. He perched next to her, his toes barely touching the roof's edge. "The Choir's keeping everything in regards to Lucifer very quiet."

"And what about everyone else? What do the rank-and-file angels know?"

"Rumors, mostly. Only a few know that Lucifer's being put on trial, but everyone's aware that there's some kind of friction in Hell. But no one will speak of it openly. The Choir has issued decrees warning against unfounded speculation and repeatedly insisted that whatever's happening in Hell is none of our concern."

"And how much do you know?" asked Anael.

"More than most, but still not enough," said Gabriel.

"Did you know Lucifer asked me to represent him in this trial?"

Gabriel gave a shortened chuckle and smiled. "No, I didn't. But it makes sense."

Anael glanced at him out the corner of her eye, her brow furrowing. "Excuse me?"

"You're tenacious and there are few in Heaven or Hell who have a stronger will or a sharper mind. But more than that, you *know* Lucifer in ways that no one else does."

"No, I don't. I don't think anyone really knows him."

"Not so sure about that."

Anael huffed. "Just because we slept together eons ago doesn't mean jack. He's not the same person he used to be, Gabriel."

Gabriel looked down at his hands as he rubbed them together. "I don't know that I can agree with you. Unlike you, I'm the only angel that's had any contact with Lucifer during his time ruling Hell."

"You were just doing your job as Heaven's messenger," said Anael.

"That was just the excuse. In reality, I *wanted* to continue talking with him."

Internally, Anael was screaming at Gabriel, demanding how he could actually *want* to maintain communication with the Adversary. But externally, she was able to restrain her emotions and just ask him a very simple, "Why?"

"He's my brother. No matter what he's done or *will* do, nothing will ever change that. Michael may have been content to disown him and treat him as the ultimate embodiment of evil, but I could never resign myself to such... simplistic thinking. We're supposedly celestial beings, Anael. We consider ourselves to be above humans. And yet, they often exhibit far more complexity and diversity of thought than us."

"There are many in Heaven who'd call for your exile if they heard you talking like that."

"I've been in a position like that, fairly recently in fact," said Gabriel. "But I didn't come to talk about me, I came to talk about you and what you plan to do."

Anael shrugged. "Nothing."

"Nothing?" Gabriel repeated her response, as if testing whether or not he heard it correctly.

"If I stay clear of this and just lay low for a time, maybe the Choir will come around."

"There's a huge flaw with that plan."

"And what's that?" she asked.

"You believe that the Choir will change their mind. To do so is to admit they made a mistake and in all my time, I've never seen them do that. If the Presence is supposed to be infallible and the Choir gives voice to the Presence, then by the transitive property the Choir is also infallible."

"What about forgiveness?"

Gabriel probed Anael's eyes with his gaze. "Ask Lucifer."

Anael shook her head and looked forward. "That's different. Forgiveness needs to be preceded by an admission of guilt."

"Of course it doesn't. Forgiveness isn't part of a transaction. It's a mercy you bestow on others. You grant forgiveness based on what's in your heart, not the actions of others."

"So what are you saying? That I should help Lucifer?"

"Do you have a reason why you shouldn't?"

"I have no interest in abetting his latest attempt to escape responsibility."

"I see it differently. I think he's accepting his role, which is the purpose for this trial."

Anael's head cocked to the side. "I don't understand you, Gabriel. You're supposed to be the messenger for the Choir, and yet here you are telling me that they're fallible and that I should help their greatest adversary."

"I'm not saying anything of the sort, I'm just asking questions and discussing the situation."

"Funny how your rumination points in one direction."

Gabriel gave a shrug. "Maybe that says more about

what's in your soul as opposed to having anything to do with my words."

"If you were in my position, what would you do?"

"I'd do what *I* believed to be right," said Gabriel. "It shouldn't matter what the Choir decrees or what Lucifer feels. When all's said and done, you have to make your own choices, Anael, because you're the one who has to live with them. The question you have to ask yourself is do you believe Lucifer deserves a defense in this matter?"

Anael looked down at the streets below the tower. "It's the question I've been asking myself."

"Defending Lucifer doesn't mean you agree with his views. It just means acknowledging his right to a defense."

"Why don't you do it?" asked Anael. "You're more sympathetic to his situation than me."

Gabriel scoffed. "Oh, wouldn't *that* be a scene. Unfortunately, I can't. I'm on thin ice as is right now and the work I'm doing in Heaven is too important to risk. I'm also not as fierce or cunning as you."

"Now you're just trying to flatter me."

"Guilty."

Anael chuckled, but her somber appearance returned quickly. "Say I do this. How will the Choir react?"

"I wish I could answer that. But I doubt they'd be very happy."

"Did they really send Kushiel after us?"

"I'm not sure. Like I said, they're keeping things close to the vest. But it wouldn't surprise me at all. I also know that Uriel is not happy with the current situation. He could prove difficult, too."

"I can deal with Uriel. Kushiel is another matter," said Anael. "Would he be able to follow us into Hell?"

"In the past, I would have said no. But the old rules don't seem to apply. I don't know what to think anymore. We can't really trust our old symbols of authority, so we have to rely on what we think is right."

"We're angels, we're not built for that."

"No, we're absolutely not. But what other choice do we have?" asked Gabriel. "I don't envy the burden that's been placed on you, Anael. If I could, I would change places with you just to relieve you of it."

"Liar," she replied with a smirk.

Gabriel laughed. "You're stepping on my moment." He sighed. "But this has to be your decision. I think we're coming to a turning point very soon and the choices we make now will be extremely influential."

His wings expanded and lifted Gabriel from his perch. He turned and faced Anael one final time. "This will probably be the last time we speak for a while. I'll try to see what I can learn about Kushiel's deployment and whether or not the Choir is really behind it. If I find out anything useful, I'll get word to you somehow."

"Thank you, Gabriel," said Anael. "I appreciate having someone in my corner."

Gabriel placed a finger to his lips. "I'm not in anyone's corner, Anael. I serve the Choir and simply act as their messenger. Any insinuations to the contrary would be wildly irresponsible."

He punctuated his remarks with a wink and then wrapped himself in his wings. Gabriel was consumed in a bright, blue light that built to a massive flash, then suddenly vanished, taking him with it.

Anael looked back over the city. The conversation with Gabriel had helped her put things into perspective. She still wasn't completely sure what she should do, but she felt more confident that she now had the tools to make the right choice.

CHAPTER 8

The most important part of a trial is not the time spent in court, it's what comes before. Preparing the case to be presented is what matters the most in any trial. But in a case like this, where there were no real laws governing the procedures—or even the crime that was at the center—made this far more challenging than any other.

Lucifer was joined in his preparations by Belial and Mara, both of whom put their regular lives on hold to help. Grant and Moore remained flies on the wall, observing everything but providing no input of their own. The Morningstar was suspicious of the pair. He understood the rationale for a neutral third party to monitor him, but Lucifer still wasn't sure that Purgatory was truly neutral. Thanatos had some sort of agenda in this, and Lucifer couldn't be certain if it were in his favor or not.

The knock on the door came as a surprise to everyone gathered. Belial gave a look in Lucifer's direction and he nodded. The demon went to the front door and opened it, surprised to see the figure standing on the other side.

"Hello, Belial," said Anael. "May I come in?"

Belial gave another glance in Lucifer's direction. The Morningstar had heard her voice and waved, a gesture for

Belial to let her in. Belial did so, stepping to the side and holding the door open for Anael.

"Thank you," she said.

Belial offered no response, just closed the door. He stayed a few paces behind her as she walked into the library and Lucifer rose from his chair to greet her.

"I wasn't expecting to see you again after our last encounter," he said.

"Neither was I," said Anael. "I spoke with Gabriel."

"Oh?"

"He doesn't know what the situation is with Kushiel, or if he does, he can't say anything. But we also spoke about your…situation."

"What did he say?" asked Lucifer.

"The details aren't important. All you need to know is that I'm here to offer my assistance."

"Convenient," muttered Mara.

Anael turned her gaze from Lucifer to the demon. "What was that?"

"Just pointing out how convenient your timing is," said Mara. "You've become targeted by Heaven, and all of a sudden, you have a change of heart. Need us to protect your ass now that your feathered friends have all turned on you?"

"That's not what this is about," said Anael. "I could deal with Kushiel on my own. I'm here for my own reasons."

"And what reasons would that be?" asked Mara, rising to her feet. "My Lord, she's never been trustworthy. The sensible thing would be to throw her out and leave her to Kushiel's mercy."

"That's enough," said Lucifer. "Mara's right, the sensible thing *would* be to let you fend for yourself."

Anael scowled. "Fine. If that's the way you feel, then I'll leave."

She was about to turn, but Lucifer grabbed her wrist to stop her.

"However," he began, "no one ever accused me of being sensible."

Mara's eyes bulged. "You can't be serious. You're really going to trust her?"

"We need help," said Lucifer. "I don't know who the Infernal Court will choose to prosecute this case, but I'm certain it will be someone very cunning. Anael can see what sort of attacks are coming, because they're the same attacks she herself would bring."

"Thank you," said Anael. "What exactly is it we're looking at here?"

"The charge Raum put forward is that the Morningstar betrayed the trust of Hell's denizens," said Belial. "He said that because the Morningstar knew the truth of the Divine Choir's lie about the Presence and said nothing, he was in effect doing the Choir's bidding the whole time."

"And what proof does the other side have?" asked Anael.

"Circumstantial evidence," Belial continued. "The treaties with Heaven, the creation of Cocytus, they say all of this was done to further the Choir's goals as opposed to being for the benefit of Hell."

"Which is nonsense, of course," said Lucifer. "Everything I did was in order to prevent war."

"Put aside the question of the Presence," said Anael.

"Why?" asked Lucifer. "You don't believe it?"

"Of course I don't," said Anael.

"Even after all this?"

Anael sighed. "Just because Raum believed your delusions and broadcast them across Hell doesn't make them true."

"My Lord, I beg you to reconsider this arrangement." Mara pointed at Anael. "If she doesn't even believe your story, how will she convince a jury that you're to be trusted?"

"I don't care what Lucifer believes or doesn't believe, nor do I care what the rest of Hell believes. All of that is immaterial to the case," said Anael. "What this case is really about is whether or not you were doing the Choir's work for them."

"Do you have any ideas, Anael?" asked Lucifer.

"It's obvious that we won't have any testimony from any of the seraphim who make up the Divine Choir, and even if we did, their credibility would be suspect. There's no real direct evidence proving that you were or weren't serving Heaven's interests. So we'll need character witnesses."

"When I went to Cross with the offer to take my place, I told him everything about the Choir and their lie," said Lucifer.

"Good, that's one," said Anael.

"I will do whatever's necessary to protect the Morningstar," said Belial.

"Fanboys aren't much help." Anael glared at Mara. "Or fangirls, for that matter. There's no shortage of demons who will testify about their love for the Morningstar."

"But they've witnessed other things. Both Belial and Mara have seen my actions on Earth and how I've tried to take responsibility for what I've done," said Lucifer.

"Good, now you're thinking," said Anael. "Will Cross testify?"

Lucifer nodded. "I believe so, yes."

"This is a good start," said Anael. "If we can convince the jury that the only thing you're guilty of is trying to prevent needless carnage, we just might have a case here."

"Of course there's an x-factor involved," said Lucifer. "Who will the Court appoint to prosecute?"

CHAPTER 9

For the trial of the Devil himself, the courtroom was remarkably mundane. The only real difference from it and any courtroom one might have found on Earth was that the large windows looked out over the crimson skies of Hell.

The jury consisted of fourteen members—two from each of the realms of Hell. Only two areas were unrepresented in the jury. First was the territory controlled by Luther Cross, and that was because he was the only inhabitant of that realm. The other was the Badlands, the stretches of desolate area between realms. They were ungoverned and thus considered to be outside the jurisdiction of the Infernal Court.

The members of the Court itself were seated together, across from the jury. Together, they decided on the manner this trial would take. It was the first time any such thing had been attempted in Hell's history, so they were all in virgin territory.

Lucifer and Anael sat together at the defense table. The gallery behind them consisted of several of Hell's denizens. But though not all could fit in this courtroom, the trial was being broadcast all across the different realms for every demon to watch.

Both Lucifer and Anael noted the absence of both the trial judge and the prosecutor. It was certainly a cause for some concern—just what was taking them so long to show up? And who exactly did the Court appoint for both those positions?

The doors to the courtroom were flung open and all heads turned to see the arrival. A tall figure clad in a red suit strode in with a confident gait, a cane tapping the ground with each step he took, though he seemed to have no limp of any kind. His hair was dark and long, spilling over his shoulders and down his back. He walked into court and past the gallery, then stopped at the defense table, where he took a bow.

Lucifer had to admire the irony of the situation. Not too long ago, he himself had sat in judgment of the demon appointed to prosecute him. In a normal court, this would no doubt be considered a conflict of interest. But the rules in Hell weren't as rigid.

Anael stood from her chair to greet the prosecutor. She squinted at him, trying to place where she knew him from. And then it suddenly hit her. "Asmodeus…?"

"Anael, my dear." Asmodeus gently took her hand and planted a soft kiss on her knuckles. "You haven't changed one bit since The Fall. So good to see you again."

The demon looked past her and at Lucifer. "Hello, Morningstar. Isn't this a funny coincidence?"

"You and I both know there's nothing coincidental about this," said Lucifer.

Asmodeus grinned. "Perhaps not. Promises to be a good spot of fun though, doesn't it? I'm really looking forward to seeing how this all plays out."

The demon bowed and then retired to his table. Anael took her seat and leaned towards Lucifer.

"I thought Asmodeus was dead?"

"Not dead, imprisoned."

"You mean he was in Cocytus?" asked Anael.

He just nodded.

Anael sighed. "Well, that's just great."

"Don't worry about him," said Lucifer. "It's unnerving, but that's all. We can deal with this."

"You know this is purposeful," said Anael.

"Of course it is." Lucifer glanced at the Infernal Court—specifically at Cross and Lilith. Both had their own histories with Asmodeus and there was no doubt in the Morningstar's mind that he would have been their last choice for prosecutor. The looks of dismay on their faces only confirmed his theory. This was clearly the result of Beelzebub's machinations. Lucifer had to hand it to the little insect—it was a gutsy move designed to throw him off-guard.

A demon emerged dressed in a uniform. "All rise." Everyone stood. "The first trial of the Infernal Court is now in session. The dishonorable Judge Samedi is presiding."

If Lucifer wasn't overly surprised by Asmodeus's presence, the mention of the judge's name was definitely more than enough to shock him. From the door behind the demon guard, another figure emerged. It was none other than Baron Samedi himself. The familiar skull was painted over his face. Sunglasses rested on his nose, the lens of one side missing through which his glowing, emerald eye could be seen. But rather than the top hat and tuxedo Lucifer had seen him in before, now the Baron wore a judge's robe with a powdered wig. He climbed up to the judge's bench and raised a large gavel, which he slammed down a few times.

"The sentence is death!" he shouted.

"Umm…your Honor…" said Anael, standing.

"*Dis*honor," corrected Samedi.

"Right…your Dishonor… Isn't it customary to have a trial *before* the sentencing?"

"Hmm," thought Samedi, rubbing his chin. "That seems a bit counterproductive, but I'll allow it, I suppose."

"What is this?" asked Lucifer, rising from his seat. "Baron Samedi?"

"*Judge* Samedi, actually," said the loa, tugging on his robe's collar.

"A neutral third party was needed to preside over the trial," said Lilith from the Infernal Court's box. "It was believed that one of the Loa would be sufficiently neutral. More so than even someone from Purgatory."

"But he's not neutral, he and I have a deal of our own," said Lucifer.

"Oh don't worry at all 'bout that, Lucy," said Samedi. "This won't interfere with my judgment one bit."

"Your Dishonor, if I may have a moment to confer with my client?" asked Anael.

"You wanna *talk* to your client?" asked Samedi with a cocked brow. "You sure got a funny way of doin' things, counselor."

Anael pulled Lucifer back down to his seat. "What's your problem?" she asked in a whisper. "If you did a deal with the judge, shouldn't you be *glad* that he's presiding over this case?"

"You don't know much about Baron Samedi, do you?" asked Lucifer.

"No, why?"

"Disruption and chaos are in his nature. If he's presiding over this thing, then it's going to be unpredictable," said Lucifer. "Besides, he and I have an arrangement and despite what he says, he might be doing this to work that arrangement to his advantage."

"What kind of arrangement?" asked Anael.

"He has a marker on my soul," said Lucifer.

"The Devil sold his soul?"

"Yes, I'm aware of the irony," said Lucifer.

"There's nothing we can do about it now," said Anael.

Lucifer eyed Samedi with concern. Anael didn't quite grasp the ramifications of the loa gaining possession of the Morningstar's soul. There was more to the deal than he'd told her. But if he said any more at this point, he was worried it would push her away. Her participation was already tenuous at best. If she knew what he'd done, she would think him too reckless to defend.

"So..." said the judge, clapping his hands and then rubbing them together with a toothy grin. "Shall we begin the greatest trial in celestial history or what?"

"The prosecution stands ready, your Dishonor," said Asmodeus.

"Excellent. An' how 'bout the defense?"

Anael looked at Lucifer. He supposed he didn't have any choice in the matter. The only option for him was to see this through. After all, he was the one who started this in the first place. He nodded.

"The defense is ready to proceed, your Dishonor," said Anael.

"All righty then. Mr. Asmodeus, the floor's yours, fam."

Asmodeus stood to give his opening statement. "Thank

you, your Dishonor." He stepped into the center of the courtroom and waited for all eyes to fall on him. "My fellow demons, Judge Samedi, members of the Infernal Court. I would like to draw your attention to a time several eons in the past. To a time before demons existed, when humans were *literally* nothing more than talking monkeys, and when Hell was empty. Most of the Court, the accused, and yours truly had wings of a different sort—the feathered variety. We served Heaven not only dutifully, but enthusiastically. The seraphim who made up the Divine Choir gave us our orders and told us that we were the loyal subjects of an omniscient deity. This deity has been given many names by the humans—Yahweh, Elohim, Jehovah, Allah, Shangdi, Nkosi, Maykapal, and literally hundreds more. But to the angels? We simply referred to him as the Presence.

"And we loved the Presence. Not because we felt his divine essence, but because we were *told* to love him," he continued. "As angels, we were created with one purpose in mind—to serve. We were little more than a slave caste and we knew nothing more. And so it was and would ever be. Or at least that's what we thought. Because one day, a great angel showed us a different path. Showed us that we need not just be slaves to the will of an absent king."

Asmodeus pointed his cane in Lucifer's direction.

"*That* angel, to be specific. He held a special place of reverence for all of us. Michael was feared, Gabriel was respected, but Lucifer? Lucifer was *loved*. He was the most beautiful of us, and the most learned. We saw him as a teacher, for his name literally means Light-Bringer. And then one day, he taught us about the concept of free will.

"He showed us through his actions that we didn't have to serve the Presence. That we could forge our own destiny.

And so, we did. All founding members of the Infernal Court served as his lieutenants. We fought a rebellion on his behalf. And we lost. The seraphim gave us all a choice—repent and denounce the Adversary, or follow him into damnation. We chose damnation."

Asmodeus paused for effect. He lowered his head and remained silent, as if trying to find the words to continue.

"On that first day in Hell, the Morningstar spoke to us all. He gave a rousing speech, proclaiming infamously that it was better to rule in Hell than serve in Heaven. And we thought we were headed towards a bright new future.

"But then came the compromises," said Asmodeus. "As the humans evolved, we attempted to exert influence on them. The first hybrids were born—the cambions were the offspring of man and demon and the Nephilim the offspring of man and angel.

"But the Nephilim became unstable. And Lucifer made his first compromise, joining with the Choir to eliminate their threat. More compromises followed and it wasn't long before Lucifer constructed the infernal prison called Cocytus. He'd followed the example of the angels and allowed them to impose their will on him—and by extension, all of us.

"This, my friends, is what the Morningstar stands accused of. For all his talk of knowledge and freedom, he imprisoned us, his own kind, in order to maintain peace with those who betrayed him. Even now, he sits with them—he's even being represented in this very trial by an angel.

"But the greatest sin of all? He *lied* to us!" Asmodeus spat that last sentence with such vitriol, it would be hard for anyone to argue that it was anything other than genuine. "He learned the *truth*! That the Presence was simply a fictional construct created by the Divine Choir in order to control us! It's a fiction they then went on to foist upon the tribes of man. To this day, the humans slaughter and persecute each other on a daily basis in the name of a deity that does not and has never existed.

"Lucifer knew this was all a lie. He knew the very foundation of Heaven was pure deceit. But he never told us the truth. For eons, he maintained the Choir's secret. And it was only through the tireless efforts of a great hero by the name of Raum that we learned of Lucifer's role in perpetuating this deception.

"My fellow demons, we have been lied to for far too long. We have been suckered into worshipping two false idols—first the Presence and then the Morningstar. And now is our opportunity to not only free ourselves of these fictions, but to extract the vengeance we've so rightfully earned on at least one of the architects of our continued humiliation.

"What we are asking of the court is to pass judgment on the Morningstar. To see to it that he suffers the way he has made others suffer. He has lied, he has deceived, he has punished. And he deserves the same treatment by a significant magnification.

"Thank you."

Asmodeus gave a bow and the gallery erupted in applause. Even the judge was clapping. Lucifer glanced at the Infernal Court and saw the looks of smug appreciation on the faces of Beelzebub, Leviathan, and Mammon.

"Suddenly, I'm starting to think this may have been a bad idea," he whispered to Anael.

"What tipped you off?" she asked, making no effort to disguise her sarcasm.

CHAPTER 10

Samedi applauded along with the rest of the court once Asmodeus completed his opening statement. The celebratory atmosphere went on for another few moments, but it felt like an eternity. Anael knew going into this that the deck would be stacked against them, but she wasn't expecting it to be this extreme. She cast a glance at the Infernal Court's box, where Luther Cross's brow furrowed as he watched the proceedings.

Finally, the applause ceased. "Gonna be tough to follow that one," said Samedi before he addressed Anael. "You sure you still wanna try your hand at this game, little angel?"

Anael rose defiantly and took center-stage. Boos and jeers came from the crowd, but she ignored them. She faced the jury and her wings emerged from her back, expanding to their full span. That simple gesture silenced the entire court.

"I know none of you like me. More than a few of you are probably wishing that you could kill me where I stand," she said. "And perhaps an angel is the last one who should speak in defense of a man who is considered to be a pawn of Heaven. Surely, doesn't my mere presence here prove Lucifer's guilt?

73

"If you believe that, then you're just as likely to believe the drivel that you just heard from Asmodeus."

Asmodeus leaned back in his chair and crossed his legs, smiling at her characterization of his statement.

"You heard a lot about how Lucifer subjugated himself before the Divine Choir. But what you didn't hear was what exactly he sacrificed in the first place," said Anael. "Asmodeus was right about one thing, Lucifer was the most beloved and revered of all the angels. In Elysium, where hierarchy is everything, he held a special rank. He wanted for nothing. Not friendship, nor comforts—" she paused for a breath before she said the next words, "—nor even love. He lived a perfect existence and he could have kept on living that way, if only he played by the rules.

"But he didn't. Lucifer was, above all things, a seeker of knowledge—of truth. No angel had a more inquisitive nature than he and when these strange being started appearing on Earth—seemingly made in the same image as us angels, but so much more frail—Lucifer found something intriguing about them. What had completely set us apart from the beasts of the Earth up until that point was the fact that we angels possessed souls. We considered it the touch of the Presence's divine will that made us that way. But when it was discovered that humans also had this spark as we called it, that raised questions. And Lucifer wanted to find answers.

"His search led him to seek out an angel named Metatron, who had at one point served as the Scribe of Heaven, but who had since gone missing. It was from him that Lucifer learned the truth, that the Presence was a lie conceived and perpetuated by the Divine Choir. Asmodeus would have you believe that Lucifer kept this knowledge to himself because he wanted to serve the Choir. But the truth of the matter is he *did* try to tell others, such as myself.

"I didn't believe him. Nothing could have ever convinced me that the Presence wasn't real."

Anael gauged the facial reactions of the jury. While at first, they were enraged by her very presence, now their expressions had softened. They were watching her with rapt attention, proving that her words were piercing through the thick layer of prejudice.

"Lucifer knew that if the Presence were a lie, then angels had no reason to be subservient to the seraphim. But angels are hierarchical. We follow orders and we were incapable of grasping the concept of free will. Lucifer sought to destroy this notion, by using humanity as his weapon. He cast a spell that fanned the spark in mankind, essentially elevating their consciousness."

"Lucifer was punished for this transgression. The Choir feared what this would represent and so they imprisoned him. And from there came the rebellion and eventually, The Fall.

"But what came next is important. Lucifer had seen firsthand the death and destruction that came from his actions and he wanted to ensure it never happened again. In the intervening years, he was faced with challenges. There was a shaky armistice with Heaven. But Lucifer knew that if there was another war, then Heaven would obliterate his little contingent. Hell was small and lacked the overwhelming might that Heaven possessed—and that situation still remains somewhat true. If Lucifer was to keep his people safe, he had only one option left to him—diplomacy.

"What Asmodeus calls subjugation, I call diplomatic maneuvering. Lucifer had to find ways to keep Heaven satisfied with the status quo. Sometimes that meant imprisoning certain individuals who stirred up trouble for their own benefit."

Anael made a point to cast a glare in Asmodeus's direction when she said that line.

"But through it all, Lucifer's only goal was to keep the best interests of his people in mind. He separated himself, dwelling on his own personal failures and constantly questioning whether he could have done something different. And so, when the opportunity came, he chose to retire.

"What you're going to hear in this trial isn't a story about a willing puppet or even a useful idiot. You're going to hear the story of an angel who sacrificed everything for all of you." She gestured at the people sitting in the room with both hands. "He—"

"Died for our sins?" chimed in Asmodeus, with a quip that drew laughter from the court.

Anael knew he was trying to get a rise out of her, to rattle her, but she refused to take the bait. "He gave up everything for all of you, and in return he's been vilified. Painted as the universe's greatest monster. Labeled Devil and Adversary and Beast.

"By the time this trial has concluded, there are two things that will be made very obvious. The first is that Asmodeus is a lying piece of shit, more concerned with satisfying his own vindictive urges. The second is that the Morningstar has spent his entire existence striving only to serve his people, be they in Heaven or Hell. And he has earned his rest.

"That's all, thank you."

Anael retracted her wings and returned to her table beside Lucifer. There was no raucous applause like there had been after Asmodeus's statement, nor a chorus of invectives as when Anael had first stood. Just an uncomfortable and contemplative silence that fell over the court.

The silence was broken by Samedi, who pounded his gavel. "We're gonna take a break, 'cuz the judge has some cravings that need satisfyin'. When we reconvene, the prosecution can present their case."

With the courtroom cleared, Anael and Lucifer retired to a private room that had been set aside for them to discuss their strategy going forward. Belial and Mara were already waiting for them when they entered.

"What the fuck was that?" asked Mara. "You call that a defense?"

"Good to see you again as well," said Anael as she took her seat at the table that had been provided.

Mara slammed her fist on the table and leaned over it. "You're supposed to be defending the Morningstar!"

"That's what I'm doing," said Anael.

"You're making him look like an incompetent failure when he's always been a strong leader! Sire, you can't keep her on. Allow me to stand up for you instead and I swear to you, I'll—"

"Guarantee his conviction?" asked Anael. "If you argue based on Lucifer's mythic status, you're going to lose. Asmodeus is counting on that and he will tear it apart."

"This right here is why I wanted someone critical of me standing up there," said Lucifer. "Anael's right, we can't fight this battle on the basis of myth. We have to argue on fact. And the fact of the matter is I *have been* an incompetent failure. I made mistakes—many of them. If the people of Hell want to hold me to account for that, then they have the right. But I *won't* be labeled a puppet."

"I'm simply trying to look out for your best interests, my lord," said Mara.

"And I appreciate that, but I've made my decision. Anael has my full faith and trust. If you want to support me, then I suggest you do the same."

Mara moved away from the table and cast her gaze towards the ground before giving a simple nod.

"Thank you." Lucifer looked at Belial. "What do you think so far? Have you heard any rumblings from the audience?"

"I was monitoring everyone during the trial. Asmodeus is a born showman and he proved how easily he can manipulate an audience," said Belial. "But Anael's statement clearly weighed on many."

"That's the impression I got as well," said Lucifer. "Would you both excuse us? I'd like to confer with my lawyer in private."

"As you wish," said Belial, moving for the exit. Mara followed him, averting her eyes from Anael's gaze.

"I have to say," Lucifer began once they were alone, "for someone who doesn't believe my story, you were quite convincing. I don't suppose you've come around?"

"Of course not," said Anael. "It doesn't matter whether or not your story about the Presence is true, all that matters is you *believe* it to be, and that's what led to your actions. If we can convince them of that, we might just have a chance at this. Though the choices of judge and prosecutor were unexpected."

Lucifer grumbled. "I suppose I shouldn't have put it

past Beelzebub to be so underhanded. First he betrays me to Raum, now this."

"He's out for blood," said Anael. "Regardless of the outcome of this trial, you should tread carefully around him."

Lucifer took a seat across the table from Anael.

"What about Samedi?" she asked. "How does he factor into this? And your deal with him?"

"I told you already, I'm not prepared to discuss that," said Lucifer. "Suffice to say, Samedi is an agent of chaos. I imagine this has more to do with him amusing himself than any other reason."

Anael scoffed and shook her head. "You always were a terrible liar. At least that will make you look honest when you get up on that witness stand."

"Well, at least my incompetence is good for something," said Lucifer.

Anael frowned. "You know it wasn't my intention to disparage you in my statement."

"Relax, I was joking," said Lucifer. "You're doing what you have to do, and I'm sure it's not easy, defending someone whom you have such mixed feelings about."

Anael sighed. "There are no *mixed feelings*. I'm simply doing what I have to. What I believe is right. Regardless of how I feel about you or the actions you've taken in the past, I certainly don't believe you should be punished for a crime you never committed."

"With any luck, maybe the jury will feel the same," said Lucifer.

"It's not going to be easy," said Anael.

"Just be ready for the unexpected," said Lucifer. "Asmodeus is going to pull every underhanded trick in the book, and a few that aren't. And it's not like there are any set rules for a case like this. Anything can and probably will happen."

"I can handle him," said Anael. "I'm not afraid of the likes of Asmodeus. Never have been, never will be."

"Maybe you should be," said Lucifer. "When he has vengeance on his mind, there's not a lot he won't do. You should ask Luther Cross about just what lengths Asmodeus was willing to go to when they fought."

"You should be ready yourself. Asmodeus is going to dredge up some uncomfortable truths about yourself. And I won't lie to you, so will I. And neither of us are going to go easy on you."

Lucifer took a breath and nodded. "Good." He met Anael's eyes with his own. "That's why I wanted you. You can't hold anything back. Only the complete, unvarnished truth will win this case."

CHAPTER 11

Once the trial had reconvened, Asmodeus stood to call his first witness, Beelzebub. The stocky, insectoid demon's gossamer wings hefted him above the box where he sat with the rest of the Infernal Court and carried him across the courtroom to the witness stand beside Samedi. Beelzebub fell abruptly and twitched his spindly arms as Asmodeus moved up to the box.

"Raise your arm, witness," said Samedi and Beelzebub did. "Do you swear to tell the truth, the whole truth, and nothing but the truth?"

"Hell no," said Beelzebub.

The judge gave a shrug. "Good enough f'r me. Any objections?"

"Yes, I absolutely obj—" Anael began.

Samedi silenced her with a bang of his gavel. "Excellent! You may proceed, counsellor."

"Lord Beelzebub, if it pleases the court, please tell us your current status," said Asmodeus.

"I'm one of the eight remaining Lordzz of Hell and a member of the Infernal Court."

"What do you mean by 'remaining'?" asked Asmodeus.

"Initially, there were nine. But that wuzz before Lucifer

81

exiled our brother, Abraxas."

Asmodeus looked crestfallen by that statement, which caused Anael to roll her eyes. He knew well and good the story of Abraxas's exile—Asmodeus himself was part of the plot to oust him. But the demon was a born actor.

"We'll revisit the tragedy of our dearly departed brother later, my Lord," said Asmodeus. "What were you before you became a Hell Lord?"

"I wuzzz an angel, in service of Heaven. My task wuzz to monitor the beasts of Earth. In particular, the Divine Choir had a keen interest in the emerging beasts that were known as humanity."

"And did the defendant ever visit you while you were working in this capacity?"

Beelzebub nodded. "He did."

"Please, relate the events of that day to us."

"In my duties, I observed signs that these creatures possessed a spark, which could indicate the presence of souls. I had reported this to the Choir and in return, they dispatched both Michael and Lucifer."

"So the Choir knew of humanity's spark and specifically sent Lucifer to observe?"

"Correct."

Asmodeus rubbed his chin. "Interesting…so Lucifer's first trip on Earth was at the behest of the Choir, who knew he would discover these ensouled creatures there. What happened next?"

"Lucifer insisted we perform a spell of sight. We did and he quickly learned that humanity did indeed pozzzess souls."

"And then?"

"They returned to Heaven. I would not see Lucifer

again until Abraxas gathered us to free him from Gehenna."

"So you joined the rebellion. Why?"

"Lucifer had returned to Earth once more, but I wuzz not witness to this. Azzz it had been relayed to me, he performed an arcane spell which ignited the spark in humanity. What I saw in monitoring theez humans wuzz a new form of being, without the need to serve the Choir. It intrigued me. And Lucifer made us believe that we could all be free of the Choir's yoke."

"In other words, you believed Lucifer when he told you he would stand against the Choir on behalf of your rights, yes?"

"Yes."

"Interesting, no further questions." Asmodeus turned and began to walk back to the table. But he stopped mid-stride and spun on his heel. "Actually, just one more if you don't mind. Did Lucifer ever once mention to you that he'd learned there was no Presence?"

"No," said Beelzebub.

"No?" Asmodeus repeated for confirmation. "Never told you that the Choir had been using the Presence as a tool for keeping you enslaved to their will?"

"Never in all the eonnzzz I faithfully served his will in Hell," said Beelzebub.

"That's very interesting. Thank you, my Lord, you've been most helpful." Asmodeus gave a bow and then returned to his seat.

"Okay, so that's that." Samedi banged the gavel. "Suppose we can move on to the sentencing now, right?"

"Your honor—"

"*Dis*honor."

Anael took a breath. "Your *dis*honor, aren't I allowed to question the witnesses as well?"

Samedi cocked one eyebrow and lowered the other. "You mean *you* get to ask questions, too?"

She sighed. "Yes. That's how a trial works."

"Well excuuuuse me, missy," said Samedi. "Not all of us went to celestial law school like *you* apparently did."

"May I question the witness?" asked Anael.

"Oh fine, I guess so." Samedi gave a wave of his hand and then propped his feet up on his box while leaning back in his chair.

Anael stood and approached the Hell Lord. "Beelzebub—"

"That's *Lord* Beelzebub," he said. "I served faithfully in the rebellion. I believe I've earned the right to be referred to by my title."

"He's got a point, *chere*," said Samedi.

"My apologies. *Lord* Beelzebub, there is a hierarchy in Heaven, is there not?"

"I've not been to Heaven in some time, I do not know how they run things theez dayzz."

"But when you were there, was there or was there not a hierarchy?"

"There wuzz."

"The angels are divided into different classes, known as choirs. At the top is the seraphim, or the Divine Choir, yes?"

Beelzebub nodded.

"Beneath that there are the archangels, and then on down the line, yes?"

"Yes."

"So…which choir were you in?" asked Anael.

"I wuzz a grigori, if memory servezz."

"Grigori…is this a high rank?"

Beelzebub did not answer right away. Anael stepped closer and cupped her hand to her ear.

"I'm sorry, I don't believe I caught your answer. Is grigori a high rank?"

"…Middle rank."

"Middle rank, I see," said Anael. "So…would it be fair to say that as Hell Lord, you hold a higher position now than you ever did in Heaven?"

Beelzebub cocked his head to the side. "Yes…"

"When Lilith and her consort, Luther Cross, sought to take over an abandoned realm, you objected, correct?"

"Yes, but what does that have to do—"

"Thank you," she interjected, not allowing him to finish his thought. "If you didn't want Cross on the Court, it stands to reason you also would not have been thrilled by his ascension to Lucifer's throne."

"Theez questions are ridi—"

"Moving on, you said you served the Morningstar faithfully for eons, correct?"

Beelzebub was starting to fume in his seat. "Will you permit me to answer this time?"

Anael nodded.

"Thank you. Yes, I served him without question."

"Fairly recently, he came to your realm and asked for your aid and you welcomed him into your kingdom, provided him with transport and protection across the Badlands. Is that all true?"

"Of course, I would have done anything the Morningstar asked of me."

Anael moved closer to the witness box. She leaned

against the edge and her face was inches from the demon's massive eyes. "But you weren't helping him, were you? In reality, you were working against him. You had allied with a would-be usurper named Raum."

"He had betrayed us."

"Did you know the truth of the Presence when you betrayed the Morningstar?"

"That's not the point!" Beelzebub's wings raised him from his seat.

"Oh it is, because it continues a clear pattern," said Anael. "You joined the rebellion because you wanted a higher station. You served Lucifer because you wanted to climb the ladder, so to speak. But when he chose to retire, he didn't name you, his loyal subject, as his successor. Instead, he chose some upstart half-breed. And what's worse, he told this new guy the truths that he never told you."

"What are you insinuating, woman?" asked Beelzebub.

"You were only interested in yourself, Beelzebub. And when you weren't given the recognition and the station you so desperately craved, you couldn't take it. You say Lucifer betrayed you and yet *you're* the one who betrayed him for your own selfish desires."

"I gave him *everything!* And he leavezzz it all to Abraxas's bastard!"

"I believe that settles it," said Anael. "No further questions."

She turned and began to walk back to the table. But Beelzebub had other ideas. His rage had overtaken him and he conjured a hellfire spear that he threw in Anael's direction.

The angel wouldn't be caught unawares. She turned and held up her hand. Her cobalt eyes crackled with divine power and held the spear in midair. Azure flames appeared around her hand as her wings emerged from her back. The spear vibrated in the air, struggling to maintain position. Slowly, the yellow hellfire began to turn blue, Anael's power taking command of the weapon. The pointed end now shifted to the opposite side. Anael locked eyes with Beelzebub and the spear flew right back at him, striking him square in the center of his body. Beelzebub crashed to the floor, alive but unconscious.

"Objection, your dishonor. She's...*spearing* the witness!" shouted Asmodeus.

"Yeah, she did at that. Seems things is heatin' up in this bitch, huh?" said Samedi, staring down at Beelzebub's prone form. He looked back at Asmodeus and cracked a smile. "Imma allow it."

"Thank you, your dishonor." Anael glanced at Asmodeus and smirked. "Your witness, counselor."

CHAPTER 12

Asmodeus was clearly unamused by Anael's tactics, but if they rattled him, he did a great job of hiding it. Once Samedi asked him to call his next witness, Asmodeus summoned Lilith to the stand.

"Isn't she on your side?" Anael whispered to Lucifer. "Would this be a good or bad development?"

"I really don't know. Lilith's alliance with me is more out of necessity than want," he replied.

Anael leaned back in her chair. "This should be interesting…"

"Mistress Lilith," said Asmodeus. "Please inform the court of how you became a demon."

"I was a human and I fell in love with a Hell Lord," said Lilith, eyeing Asmodeus with disdain. "I wasn't very smart in those days."

Asmodeus ignored the slight. "And what did this union lead to?"

"The first of the cambions, offspring of humans and demons."

"Demons and humans choosing to love one another, that would seem to be an act of free will, would it not?" asked Asmodeus.

Lilith paused before answering. Anael watched with rapt attention. Asmodeus was obviously baiting a trap and there was no doubt that Lilith was as aware of this fact as Anael.

"Would you like me to repeat the question, Mistress?" asked Asmodeus.

"You here to answer questions, girlie. Best you get to it," said Samedi.

"Yes, I suppose it could be interpreted that way," said Lilith.

"And Lucifer claimed to do everything in the service of free will, yes?"

"I wasn't part of the rebellion, so I don't know what he said back then. Anything I've heard would thus be construed as hearsay."

Asmodeus smirked. She wasn't going to make this easy on him and it was clear he found that amusing.

"What was the celestial reaction to your children?" asked Asmodeus.

"They were met with disdain," said Lilith. "Even demons felt they were inferior half-breeds and abominations." Her eyes drifted to the Infernal Court. "I believe Beelzebub had some choice phrases about them."

"The Lord Beelzebub is not the one on trial here. Now tell us, Mistress, what was the reaction in Heaven?"

"My understanding is that they were angered. I was executed and my soul sent to Hell."

"And once there, what became of you?"

"I was the the first demon born as human."

"And did Lucifer welcome you with open arms?"

Lilith's eyes glanced in Lucifer's direction.

"M'lady?"

"No, he didn't," she said. "I was imprisoned."

"I see. And why?" asked Asmodeus.

"Imprisoning me was seen as a way to appease Heaven, an olive branch to calm hostilities," she said.

"So Lucifer, paragon of free will, chose to punish you for exercising that free will. All so he could appease the forces of Heaven. Does that sound about right?"

"I can't say for certain what his motivations were," said Lilith.

"Let's fast-forward to recent events. You found a way to escape Hell, did you not?"

"Yes. I had been trapped in the realm of a Hell Lord who vanished and I was now able to escape. I traveled to Earth and joined forces with a cambion named Luther Cross."

"And what was your plan?"

"The Hell Lord had been my husband and I wanted to stake my claim to his territory."

"And Lucifer was happy to accept this, yes?"

Lilith took a breath. "He required some…convincing."

"Because doing so would upset the Divine Choir, correct?" asked Asmodeus.

"I don't kn—"

"Thank you, Mistress. No further questions."

Asmodeus returned to his seat and sat in his chair, then propped up his legs on the table. Anael stood and rested her hands on her own table.

"Mistress, who was your husband? This Hell Lord who seduced you when you were a human?"

"Asmodeus," said Lilith.

"The counselor? Very interesting. The counselor's argument hinges on the idea that Lucifer feared to stand against

Heaven, which ran counter to the wishes of the denizens of Hell," said Anael.

"Your Dishonor, is there a question somewhere in her rambling?" asked Asmodeus as he examined his nails.

"I'm getting to it, if your Dishonor would just allow me some time to set the stage," said Anael.

Samedi shrugged. "Hurry it along, child. We may got an eternity, but don't mean I want it to take that long."

"Thank you." Anael turned her attention back to Lilith. "Did Asmodeus object to Lucifer's choice?"

"No," she said.

"Objection!" shouted Asmodeus.

"On what grounds?" asked Anael.

"On the grounds of...of..." Asmodeus struggled to find a reason. "Of being a catty bitch."

"You can't object just because you don't like what I'm saying," said Anael.

"An' I got a soft spot for catty bitches anyways," said Samedi. "Go on, girl."

"Asmodeus didn't object to Lucifer's decision. He didn't fight back?" asked Anael.

"Not even a little," said Lilith.

"And in whose realm were you kept confined?"

"Asmodeus's," said Lilith.

"And when Asmodeus finally did return, how did he react to your new position?"

"He tried to kill me."

"So for all his talk that Lucifer went against you just because it was what Heaven wanted, he himself saw no problem with the arrangement at the time. Seems rather convenient that his position has now changed," said Anael. "No further questions."

The next witness Asmodeus called was himself. Anael stood to object, but Lucifer placed a hand on her arm before she was able to speak. The angel glanced down at him in surprise and Lucifer just smiled at her.

"Let him go on," said Lucifer. "Give him enough rope to hang himself and then you get to cross-examine him."

"Somethin' you were gonna say, counselor?" asked Samedi as Asmodeus stepped up to take the stand.

"Nothing, your Dishonor." Anael sat back down and then leaned over to Lucifer and whispered to him. "Hope you're right about this."

"Trust me, I am," said Lucifer.

What followed was a somewhat surreal scene in which Asmodeus would ask questions and then answer them himself. Most of it was all about the sense of betrayal he felt when Lucifer had given his realm over to Cross and Lilith. He also spoke of his hurt when Lucifer provided Cross with the means to imprison Asmodeus within Cocytus.

It was all total nonsense, but Asmodeus loved to put on a show. Lucifer meanwhile scribbled a few notes that he slid over to Anael.

As far as Lucifer was concerned, the trial couldn't have been going better. Beelzebub's testimony had been the most damaging, but Anael did a marvelous job of painting him as a shameless opportunist. And despite the attempts to use Lilith against him, Asmodeus only made himself look bad. As Anael had pointed out, Asmodeus was all too happy to throw his wife under the bus for his own well-being.

At the rate things were going, Lucifer would come out this trial with more support from the people of Hell.

Beelzebub and his co-conspirators on the Infernal Court wouldn't be too happy, but he could leave all this behind in short order.

While Lucifer considered his own thoughts, Asmodeus had finished questioning himself. It was Anael's turn now and Lucifer focused his attention on her when she stood for questioning.

"Counselor, I just have a few questions for you," said Anael. "To begin with, during your reign as a Hell Lord, where did you spend most of your time?"

"What do you mean?" asked Asmodeus.

"Where were you, physically? Here in Hell or somewhere else?"

"I was on Earth," he said.

"Earth? Why is that?"

"To spread the message of the Morningstar. To serve as a front in the ongoing conflict with Heaven."

"So you despise Heaven?" asked Anael. "Does the name Eden sound familiar?"

Asmodeus tipped his head, resting his fingers on his temple. "Yes, it's an outpost for Heaven."

"Until recently, I'd been assigned there."

"Good for you, but I don't see how that's relevant to me."

"Every time a being enters Eden, their presence is logged. Think of it as a kind of celestial security system. And I had access to these logs," said Anael. "During the time when Raziel served as the ambassador running Eden, you visited on average about once a week."

The slight flaring of Asmodeus's nostrils was the only indication of his annoyance. In all the time Lucifer had known the demon, he would be hard-pressed to think of an instance when someone got under his skin this much.

"I regularly visited Eden in order to maintain an open channel of communication with our enemies. Even in times of war, both sides must have a way to talk with each other."

"And you worked alongside Raziel and Luther Cross to protect a nephilim child, didn't you?" asked Anael.

"That's an oversimplification of the situation."

"Then please, explain your reasoning," said Anael.

"There was a rogue angel involved in creating nephilim, which posed a clear and present danger to Hell."

"So you put aside your differences with an angel because there was a greater threat that existed," said Anael. "In other words, the situation was more complex than it seemed on its surface."

"Very good, I knew you could understand if I explained it in simple words."

Anael sneered at his condescension. "Then how is it any different from the Morningstar keeping his own people in check to avoid unnecessarily antagonizing Heaven?"

"It's very different," said Asmodeus.

"So you wouldn't have imprisoned your own wife in Hell to appease Heaven?"

"Of course not."

"But you went along with it," said Anael. "You never challenged Lucifer, did you?"

"I didn't feel it was my place," said Asmodeus.

"So Lucifer made all the decisions?" asked Anael. "Unilaterally, with no room for dissent?"

Asmodeus looked away from Anael, turning his head back and staring at the ceiling. Lucifer grinned. She'd backed Asmodeus into a corner and there was nothing he could do other than admitting defeat.

Anael wouldn't relent and stepped closer to the witness box. "Well, Asmodeus? Did Lucifer make Hell's decisions unilaterally, yes or no?"

Asmodeus grunted and mumbled something.

"I'm sorry, I didn't quite catch that." Anael cupped a hand over her ear. "Say it a bit louder."

"The Court voted on all decisions," said Asmodeus.

"I see. And were there ever votes when members of the Court dissented from Lucifer?"

Asmodeus didn't vocalize his response, but just nodded.

"So you had the opportunity to object when the choice was made over what to do with Lilith. In that case, I assume you voted in favor of her freedom, correct?"

Asmodeus went silent once more. Anael glanced at the judge. "Your Dishonor, could you instruct the witness to answer the question?"

"You want them to answer your questions, you gotta answer hers, too," said Samedi. "You put yourself on that stand, boy."

Asmodeus huffed. "I voted with the Morningstar."

"Thank you," said Anael. "No further questions."

Asmodeus stepped down from the stand and walked passed the angel. As he did, he whispered a remark to her. "Don't think I'll forget this."

Anael returned to her seat and Lucifer leaned over to whisper into her ear. "You certainly rattled him. I think that may have been your finest performance so far."

"Better than spearing Beelzebub?" she asked.

"Well…maybe not *better*, but certainly more effective."

"So that's that. Asmodeus, you got any other witnesses to call?" asked Samedi.

"Just one," said Asmodeus as he returned to his table. He stared at Anael and smiled. "Prosecution calls the angel to the stand."

CHAPTER 13

Lucifer and Anael were both taken aback when Asmodeus called her to the stand. Was this always what the demon had planned or was he just lashing out in revenge after Anael humiliated him? The answer probably lay somewhere in the middle.

"Objection, your Dishonor. I'm counsel for the defense, not a witness," said Anael.

Samedi gave a shrug. "Asmodeus over there's counsel for the prosecution, didn't stop him from testifyin'. You didn't object then so why now?"

Lucifer cringed. He didn't have to see Anael's eyes to know she was glaring at him. Maybe if he hadn't stopped her from objecting before, she wouldn't be stepping up to the stand now.

"I know what you're thinking," he whispered. "We have to push on. Take the stand, answer his questions, and then you'll get a rebuttal on cross."

Anael rose from her seat and took the stand. Asmodeus moved up to the witness box and rapped his fingers on its surface, taking his time before he began his questioning. Whether Anael's testimony was part of an overall strategy or not, Asmodeus making her wait like this was clearly just a petty attempt at annoyance.

"Welcome to Hell, madame angel," said Asmodeus, finally beginning his examination.

"I have a name," she replied. "I'd ask that you use it."

"As you wish." Asmodeus continued to tap his fingers on the edge of the witness box. "Among the angels, which choir do you belong to?"

"The malakim," she said.

"Those are the messengers, yes?" asked Asmodeus.

"You know they are."

"And prior to The Fall, how would you describe your relationship with the Morningstar?"

Anael glanced at Lucifer. He nodded, giving her permission to go ahead and answer the question.

"We were…close," she said.

"Being a bit coy, aren't you, naughty girl?" asked Asmodeus. "You were fucking each other, weren't you?"

Anael sneered at Asmodeus's characterization. There were chortles coming from the audience. Maybe this was all just an attempt to throw her off her game. Lucifer could only hope she wouldn't let it affect her too much. He shook his head, trying to signal to her that she shouldn't let him get the better of her.

"We were lovers, yes," said Anael.

"It's a matter of record now that the Morningstar quote-unquote 'rebelled' against the Divine Choir because he uncovered their great lie. Both sides have stipulated to this fact of the case. But my question is did you ever know about this lie before recent events?"

"I did," said Anael.

"Really?" asked Asmodeus. "I find this highly suspect. You see, I served in Lucifer's rebellion. I was one of his trusted lieutenants and later, a Lord of Hell in my own right. And yet, not once in all that time did Lucifer ever inform me or any of my compatriots of this secret."

"I neither know nor care how informed or ignorant you and your treasonous friends are, Asmodeus."

"Maybe not, but I'm simply placing this in context," said Asmodeus. "When did Lucifer first tell you of this lie?"

Anael again glanced in Lucifer's direction. Asmodeus moved in front of her, breaking her line of sight with the Morningstar.

"Don't look at him for your answers. Just speak the truth," said Asmodeus.

"He told me as soon as he learned it."

"So *you* he trusted with this information, but *not* any of his most-trusted advisors. I find that very interesting," said Asmodeus. "What was your reaction?"

"I thought he was crazy. I told him he shouldn't go down this path."

"But he didn't listen, did he?"

Anael shook her head. "No, no he didn't."

"When he didn't listen, what did you do?"

Lucifer understood now what Asmodeus was doing. This was more than just revenge for Anael embarrassing Asmodeus on the stand. Asmodeus had planned this all along. To use Lucifer's affection for Anael against him despite her own betrayal.

"I went to Michael," said Anael.

"The archangel, yes? General of the Heavenly Host?"

"Yes."

"Doesn't that seem a bit…extreme?" asked Asmodeus.

"There was no one Lucifer held in higher regard than Michael. I felt that if he spoke, Lucifer would listen."

"And how did that turn out?"

Anael sighed. "Michael informed the Choir and they ordered him to take Lucifer prisoner."

"Which he did, but not before Lucifer completed his spell awakening mankind. Thus spurring in the rest of us a desire for something more and an admiration for the Morningstar's actions," said Asmodeus. "And that, in turn, led to the rebellion and, ultimately, The Fall.

"But all of that is well-covered terrain. I'd like to focus now on more recent events. After The Fall, when was the next time you saw Lucifer?" asked Asmodeus.

"A very long time after, following his abdication of the throne."

"So what was the purpose of this meeting? You felt like checking in on an ex?" asked Asmodeus. "What had you been doing all this time?"

"I was in Heaven, serving my role as a messenger. I had very little interaction with Earth. But I was reassigned to Eden at the request of the new ambassador. Seeing Lucifer again was my assignment."

"What assignment was this?"

"To convince him to return to Hell."

Asmodeus turned from the witness box and directed his next question to the onlookers sitting in the audience. "Let's recap the situation for everyone assembled. You hadn't seen Lucifer since you betrayed him to the Choir, you never felt any remorse for having betrayed his trust, and when the opportunity to see him once again came around, you only did so because you were *ordered* to.

He turned his gaze back to the witness box. "Does that about sum it up?"

"Perhaps a bit simplistically, but yes," said Anael.

"And how did Lucifer react when he saw you?" asked Asmodeus.

The question triggered Lucifer's memory of their recent reunion. He had been in the pool when Anael appeared before him. Her attitude was one of barely restrained anger, but Lucifer felt only wistfulness for what had once existed between them.

"He was cordial," said Anael.

"*Cordial?* When Lilith birthed the first cambion, he restrained her in Hell. When Astaroth attempted to tempt the Nazarene, he imprisoned him in Cocytus. When Raum revealed the secret he'd been keeping, he vaporized him." Asmodeus had counted each of those examples on his fingers and then pointed at Anael. "But when you betray him more than any other has, he holds no grudges? Not even a harsh tone?"

Jeers started to rise up from the audience. Asmodeus seemed to feed on their negativity and he pressed on with his badgering.

"And how did *you* treat him, *angel?*" He hissed that last word. "Were you as cordial with him as he was with you?"

"No," said Anael. "I had a job to do and I intended to see it through."

"So despite the fact that you hadn't shown any remorse or even interest in the Morningstar, he still sought your approval and counsel. Even for this trial, it was *you* he went to instead of one who has always been loyal to him," said Asmodeus. "I believe that says it all, don't you?"

"You have no idea what you're talking about, demon," said Anael.

"Oh, I think I know *fully* of which I speak," said Asmodeus. "Lucifer has *always* held angels in higher regard than demons. It's why the touch of Hell *never* affected him in the way it's affected the rest of us. Because once all is said and done, Lucifer still believes himself to be an angel, to be a servant of the Divine Choir."

"That's a lie, he—"

"I'm not finished!" said Asmodeus. "He loves you still, because you are an angel. He works against demons and puts on the throne a half-breed who has spent most of his life trying to destroy us. All of this proves that Lucifer is no hero of Hell, but a puppet of Heaven."

The boos and taunts grew more extreme. Lucifer clasped his hands together and closed his eyes. He knew this trial wasn't going to be a walk in the park, but he didn't expect it to be this much of a circus. Anael had tried her best, but he doubted how much further this could last without a verdict that would prove disastrous for him.

What was even worse was he found he was doubting his own intentions after all this time. Lucifer had always told himself that every action he took was the best thing that could be done for Hell. To keep the Choir from finding some reason to turn against them all and start a new war, one that the demons would certainly lose.

But now, he was starting to believe there was some truth in Asmodeus's accusations. Lucifer had never held anything against Anael for her betrayal and he had doled out harsh punishments to those who had tried to go against the Choir without his consent. He himself had routinely refused any sort of action that would threaten the Choir's agenda, more intent on maintaining the status quo.

Maybe on some subconscious level, Lucifer indeed still thought of himself as an angel.

Once Asmodeus returned to his seat, Samedi turned his gaze down to Anael in the witness box. "He got a chance to ask himself questions, so what about you? You gonna question yourself, angel-babe?"

Judging by the expression on her face, Lucifer assumed Anael wasn't about to go down that route. She didn't exactly have Asmodeus's flair for dramatic monolog, so it was unlikely to help them anyway. But an idea came to the Morningstar, and he stood from his seat.

"Actually, I'll be the one asking the questions."

"Objection, the defendant is not a counselor," said Asmodeus.

"You're the prosecution, not a witness, but that didn't stop you," said Lucifer.

"Boy makes a convincin' argument to me." Samedi banged the gavel a few times. "I'll allow it. Your witness, Lucy baby."

"Thank you, your Dishonor."

Lucifer moved from the table in front of the witness box. Anael was watching him with anticipation, obviously wondering just what sort of questions he was about to ask. Lucifer had been wondering the exact same thing. He jumped on this opportunity spur of the moment, didn't have any sort of plan. And now he had to whip up some questions out of thin air.

"You were the first and only angel the defendant took into his confidence," Lucifer began. It felt a little strange to refer to himself in the third person, but it helped to divorce him from the questions he was asking. "I doubt the prosecution would refute that, would you, Asmodeus?"

Lucifer cast a quick glance back at Asmodeus. The demon just shrugged, which was as close to confirmation as they were likely to get.

"As far as I know, that's correct," said Anael.

"So it's fair to say that the defendant trusts you more than any other angel."

"Perhaps, you'd have to ask him."

"I have a strong suspicion he'd agree with that thesis." Lucifer grinned. "And in the time since the defendant abdicated his throne, you've had many conversations with him, haven't you?"

"I have," said Anael.

"Did the Divine Choir ever come up in those conversations?"

"A few times, yes."

"And how would you characterize the defendant's attitude towards the Choir?"

"One of disdain. He felt the Choir betrayed all the angels. He wanted nothing to do with them."

"You went to Eden on assignment from the Choir?"

"The Choir tasked the ambassador with convincing the Morningstar to return to Hell. He in turn tasked it to me."

"So the Choir's goal was for the defendant to retake the throne?" asked Lucifer.

"Yes, that's true," said Anael.

Lucifer came to the conclusion of his questioning. "In other words, the defendant felt betrayed by the Choir and refused to do the one thing they wanted him to do. Now, would you characterize all that as the behavior of a puppet?"

"No, I'd characterize it as the actions of an obstinate rebel."

"Thank you, Anael, you've been most helpful in this

matter." Lucifer returned to his seat.

But before Samedi could dismiss Anael, Asmodeus stood again. "Just a quick rebuttal if it pleases the court, your Dishonor."

Samedi shrugged. "Sure, why not?"

"Anael, you've testified that Lucifer trusts you. Perhaps more than he trusts anyone else. Is that true?" asked Asmodeus.

"As far as I know, yes," she replied.

"Now refresh my memory, who was it that betrayed Lucifer to Michael prior to The Fall?"

"I did," she said.

"You betrayed him, but he still trusts you. Interesting," said Asmodeus. "We've all just heard testimony from this witness that the defendant feels betrayed by the Divine Choir. Yet as we see from that very same witness, a sense of betrayal doesn't seem to hinder the defendant's loyalty."

Anael opened her mouth to try to respond, but Asmodeus wouldn't let her have the floor.

"I believe we've gotten all we need out of this witness, your Dishonor. And so the prosecution will now rest its case."

CHAPTER 14

Court had adjourned following the prosecution's rest. Asmodeus left the courtroom feeling confident in his chances. Lucifer may have remained beloved in Hell even following his abdication, but Asmodeus felt he was doing a great job of drilling holes in that wall of support. It would also be fitting revenge after everything he'd endured over the past few years.

First he was abandoned to Purgatory and when he finally managed to free himself, he discovered that his realm had been given to the man responsible. Lucifer allowed that to happen and then provided the means for Asmodeus to remain trapped in Cocytus. Having the opportunity to turn the screws on Lucifer and exact vengeance for these slights had now become Asmodeus's primary reason for being. And to think of all the eons he'd wasted admiring the Morningstar...

Once he secured a conviction against Lucifer, Asmodeus could then begin the next phase of his plan—to secure control over his realm and then eventually, Hell itself.

The irony of course was that he would have been content to just get his realm back after Purgatory. But the degradation he'd been subjected to had expanded his appetites.

Asmodeus had been provided with quarters located in Beelzebub's realm. It wasn't the same as the palace he once possessed in his own realm, but it would do for now. Only he was supposed to be able to enter, so imagine his surprise when he returned to find two figures waiting there for him.

Grant and Moore, the twin errand boys of Purgatory. Asmodeus knew them well from his own time spent there, and was none too happy to see them here. Hellfire started to coalesce in his hands, waiting to be unleashed.

"The fuck are you two doing here?" he growled.

"First, we must caution you against the use of violence on our persons, Mr. Asmodeus," said Grant. "Mr. Moore and I are here on a mission of diplomacy."

"Mr. Grant speaks the truth, Mr. Asmodeus. It would be incredibly poor manners to assault those who simply wish to parley with you," said Moore.

"You're working with Lucifer, what possible interest would I have in speaking to you?" asked Asmodeus.

Grant and Moore exchanged blank looks from behind their sunglasses. Then they chuckled in unison, creating a kind of bizarre echo effect.

"I'm afraid you've been misinformed, Mr. Asmodeus," said Moore. "Mr. Grant and I are not now nor have we ever been employed by the Morningstar."

"Mr. Moore and myself are extensions of Thanatos himself. We serve his will and his will alone," said Grant.

"Then why have you been by Lucifer's side?"

"A third-party was necessary to monitor the accused, that is all," said Grant.

"And as third-party arbiters, we have been instructed

to serve as a go-between with another party," said Moore.

"In short, Mr. Asmodeus, we are here to offer you a deal."

"And if we were able to offer counsel, we would advise you to take said deal, my dear sir."

"I'm certainly a fan of brokering deals." Asmodeus waved his hand and a chair moved from the corner of the room and slid across the floor until it was right behind him. He sat down in it and crossed his legs. "But I need to know more details."

Neither Grant nor Moore made a request for chairs of their own. They remained standing with their hands neatly clasped in front of them.

"How confident are you in your ability to obtain a conviction, Mr. Asmodeus?" asked Moore.

"Quite confident," said Asmodeus.

"Should a conviction be obtained, have you given any thought to the question of sentencing?" asked Grant.

"Not particularly, no."

"As you are well aware due to your own history, Hell is now without a prison, Mr. Asmodeus," said Grant.

"And death would seem more of a release than punishment," said Moore.

"What do you propose then? Purgatory?" asked Asmodeus. "I imagine Heaven wouldn't be too happy with that arrangement."

Grant and Moore both grinned at the mention of Heaven.

"It's funny you should mention Heaven, Mr. Asmodeus," said Moore.

"It just so happens that we are here to invite you to a meeting with a very interesting individual," said Grant.

Asmodeus narrowed his eyes. "Please don't tell me you're talking about an angel. The last time I got involved with one of those, it didn't work so well for me."

"All we are asking is for you to meet with him, Mr. Asmodeus," said Grant.

"It would indeed be in your best interests," said Moore.

"I doubt it."

"And, Mr. Moore, we should probably add that Mr. Asmodeus has something of an obligation…?"

"Ahh yes, that's right, Mr. Grant. After all, Mr. Asmodeus *did* make a deal with our master. One which he never lived up to."

"You can't seriously hold me to that deal," said Asmodeus. "I was sent to Cocytus!"

"Correct me if I'm wrong, Mr. Grant, but Cocytus no longer exists, does it?"

"You are most certainly *not* wrong, Mr. Moore."

Asmodeus fumed in his chair. As manifestations of Purgatory itself, even if he could kill Grant and Moore, it likely wouldn't mean their destruction. They'd simply return, like they always did. And he'd still be indebted to Thanatos.

"Very well, set up the meeting."

"We are so pleased you've agreed to see things logically, Mr. Asmodeus," said Grant.

"Yes, we shall proceed post-haste," said Moore.

"Wait, now?" asked Asmodeus. "I didn't think—"

"No time like the present, Mr. Asmodeus," said Moore.

"Early bird gets the worm and all that," said Grant.

The pair faced each other and clasped hands, moving close enough so their chests touched. They seemed to merge into one being for a brief moment and when they parted, a portal opened in the space. Asmodeus rose from his chair and approached the portal, looking through it.

He couldn't see what was on the other side. The portal seemed to lead to a black void. They made it clear that he had no say in this, so if he tried to refuse now, he wasn't sure what they would do. And he wasn't particularly curious to find out.

Asmodeus stepped into the portal and he found that on the other side there was indeed nothingness. Every bit the void that it had seemed when he peered inside. However, there was a table and two chairs on either end. One chair was already occupied by an angel in a white suit with silver hair and a beard, his wings on display, but in a resting position.

Not to be outdone, Asmodeus's own demonic wings emerged and he took the empty seat. "Hello, Uriel. It's been a dog's age."

"Asmodeus," said Uriel, though there was clear disdain in his tone. "I wish I could say that it's nice to see you again."

"Look at that, we already agree on something. Maybe this will go better than we expected." Asmodeus then looked around the void, but saw no sign of Grant and Moore. "What happened to the Olsen Twins?"

"My guess is they don't want to be party to what's being discussed. Plausible deniability and all that," said Uriel. "Now, about this trial…"

"Interesting move on Lucifer's part, eh?" asked Asmodeus. "Not quite sure what his endgame is, but I do like the opportunity it's created."

"You're not the only one interested in seeing Lucifer in chains," said Uriel. "Kushiel was dispatched to Earth to take him prisoner. It was only Purgatory's intervention that stopped him."

"And here I always assumed the Choir wanted Lucifer around."

"So long as he played his role. But if he won't sit on the throne of Hell, he can't be the Devil they need. He doesn't want to play the game anymore."

"And so they've stopped humoring him as a result," said Asmodeus. "An interesting turn of events."

"The problem is Purgatory. Thanatos has sworn that this trial must continue or else Heaven will have a two-front war on its hands," said Uriel. "The Choir also doesn't want to see another war."

"And since when do you speak for the Choir?" asked Asmodeus.

Uriel's gaze shifted towards the table. Asmodeus smiled.

"Of course," he said. "You're *not* here on the Choir's behalf, but you think you've found a way to get into their good graces."

"This trial is a black mark on my record. Lucifer's return to Hell wasn't the end we thought it would be and it's only stirred up more problems," said Uriel. "Kushiel was dispatched without my knowledge or consent."

"And if you can strike a deal that will allow the Choir to take the Morningstar prisoner, you'll be the new golden boy. I have to say, Uriel, I admire your dedication to supplicating yourself."

Uriel's eyes flashed with cobalt anger. "Watch your tongue, heretic."

Asmodeus held his hands up in a gesture of peace. "Easy now, no offense meant."

"You know the situation," said Uriel. "If Lucifer is

found guilty by Hell, there's no more Cocytus. Nowhere to imprison him. But Gehenna still exists."

"And you believe if we turn Lucifer over to Kushiel in a deal you've brokered, the Choir will give you a gold star. Yes, it's quite clear how you benefit from this." Asmodeus leaned forward, clasping his hands and resting them on the table's surface. "Now what's in it for me?"

"The Choir needs its supervillain. Hell needs its Satan. Not some vapid figurehead who broods in a tower, but someone who will prove to angels and humans alike that there is a battle between good and evil," said Uriel. "Lucifer's not willing to play that role, if he ever was. And Cross certainly isn't any better. But you?"

Asmodeus leaned back in his chair. "So I help you with Lucifer, and you help me with my pursuit of power. I rather like that idea. Only question is, how will we keep it secret?"

Uriel grinned. "You think the Choir doesn't know how to conduct secret operations? There is one catch, however."

"What's that?"

"Lucifer must not be found innocent. Not under any circumstances. Can you guarantee his conviction?"

"I think that can certainly be arranged. However, I'll need some help. You know who's representing him, don't you?"

Uriel groaned. "No, but I don't think it'd be hard to guess."

"She'll need to be dealt with. If you can work some magic on your end, then it will be easier to guarantee Lucifer's loss in court."

"Excellent." Uriel stood and held out his hand. "Then we have a deal?"

LUCIFER JUDGED

Asmodeus rose and gripped the angel's hand. They shook.

CHAPTER 15

While the trial was in recess, it gave both sides an opportunity to recuperate. Lucifer had chosen to return to his Chicago home for the time being with some of his supporters. The mood at the home was celebratory, with drinks flowing freely and music loud enough that the neighbors would eventually complain.

Lucifer sat out on the patio with a drink in one hand and a cigar in the other. Belial and Mara were also seated near him, each of them nursing their own drinks. They had invited both Cross and Lilith to join the festivities, but due to their roles in the Infernal Court, both felt it would be better that they at least attempt to appear neutral until the trial's end. Also present were Grant and Moore, standing off to the side, silently observing everything that transpired.

"Just imagine it, my friends. Once this trial ends, any responsibilities I still have to Hell will be lifted," said Lucifer.

"So you hope," added Belial in a hushed voice.

Lucifer turned his attention to his faithful lieutenant. "You don't agree?"

Belial took a sip of his drink and shook his head. "I

hope for the best, my Lord. But I would caution against overconfidence. Asmodeus is one of the craftiest demons in existence."

"Maybe so, but all you need to do is look around—Hell *loves* the Morningstar," said Lucifer.

"So did Heaven, once upon a time," added Belial.

"Ignore him, my Lord," said Mara. "Belial's not having fun unless he's tearing out someone's spine."

"I have fun..." Belial protested in a whispered voice.

"But if it does all go the way you suspect, what will you do once the trial's over?" asked Mara. "No more worries of Cocytus, no more dealing with the Court or the Choir, what will you do then?"

Lucifer gave a shrug. "I have no idea. And I find that prospect intoxicating. To be completely free of any burdens for the first time in my existence." He finished his drink and held the empty glass in front of his face. Lucifer stared at the container and his eyes pulsated with golden energy. The cup magically refilled itself and he went back to drinking.

"Of course, there is one thing I wish we had that we presently don't. The only thing truly preventing my case from being as rock-solid as I'd like is a key witness," said Lucifer. "The Scribe."

"Metatron," said Belial. "Why him?"

Lucifer nodded. "Metatron is the one who revealed the secret to me in the first place. And he learned it through the power of a spell the Divine Choir cast on him. They thought it would give him vision to help him better transcribe the history of the universe. Little did they know it would also give him the power to see through their lie."

"Where is he then?" asked Mara.

"He disappeared from Heaven eons ago, even before

the rebellion. I managed to find him in Purgatory, but since then, no one knows where he is," said Lucifer.

"Have you tried asking the Men In Black?" asked Mara, jerking her thumb over her shoulder to indicate Grant and Moore.

"I have, but they insist he's not in Purgatory any longer. Whether that's the truth is another question, but trying to press the issue with Thanatos may only cause more problems than it's worth," said Lucifer.

"Would you like me to reach out to my contacts?" asked Belial. "Perhaps Black's network…"

"If you can do so without arousing suspicion, then yes. But I don't want Black to know too much about what's happening," said Lucifer.

"You know that won't last," said Mara. "Sooner or later, word of the trial will spread up here. And…" She pointed her finger towards the sky, "…up there."

"I'm quite certain it's too late for that."

Lucifer glanced behind him and saw Anael approach their table. The other demons at the party gave her a wide berth. Though she was defending their hero, they still had a healthy dose of mistrust for any angels.

"Ah, the queen of the hour." Lucifer stood and moved to Anael's side. "Now everyone, if I can have your attention, I do have a toast to make."

"Now's really not the time," said Anael. "We have things to discuss…"

"In a minute, Ana. Let your hair down for just one night." Lucifer then directed his speech to the party. "The successes we've had in the trial thus far are all because of this woman right here. My enemies thought they could easily win this by bringing in Asmodeus or even appointing

Baron Samedi as the judge. But what they didn't count on was the tenacity and cunning of an angel. She has eviscerated his case thus far and once we present our case, I'm certain that the verdict will not be in doubt. So I'd like to ask everyone to raise a glass in honor of Anael."

Lucifer set his glass down and put his cigar in his mouth, and led the applause. Belial and Mara followed and slowly, so did the other demons. But none of them were as enthusiastic as the Morningstar. The idea of applauding an angel—even one who was helping their cause—seemed blasphemous.

"Are you done?" asked Anael. "Because like I said, we *really* need to talk."

Lucifer removed the cigar. "Fine, let's go inside." He picked up his glass and led Anael into the house. The entire first floor was filled with guests and so there was no quiet to be had there. They had to go to the second floor and out onto the master bedroom's balcony.

"There," he said as he jumped on the railing and perched. "All alone, as requested. Now could you tell me what's so important that it couldn't wait until after the party?"

"Gabriel reached out to me," said Anael.

"I know, you told me. He convinced you to change your mind."

"No, I mean after the recess began," she continued.

"He wanted to wish us well?"

Anael shook her head. "It wasn't a social call. He was delivering a message. I've been summoned, Lucifer."

Lucifer hopped off the railing. "What do you mean *summoned*?"

"You know what I mean," she said. "The Choir has requested my presence."

"What? The Choir almost never demands a direct audience. They typically work through messengers like Gabriel."

"Then consider this one of their rare exceptions," said Anael.

"Can you hold them off?"

She shook her head. "The message has been delivered. Gabriel said there's nothing he can do."

"You can't go," said Lucifer.

"I have no choice."

"You *know* the meeting is about the trial. If you appear before them, they'll forbid you from serving as my counsel."

"And what choice do I have?" asked Anael. "If I refuse to appear, it will be considered a transgression. Unlike you, I don't have Purgatory's protection if they send Kushiel after me. At least this way, I'll have an opportunity to plead my case to them, perhaps convince them that this is in the best interests of maintaining cosmic harmony."

"And what if they still command you to drop the case?"

Anael sighed. "I don't like it any more than you do. But if it comes down to that, you and I both know that I'll have no choice but to do as they command."

Lucifer turned away from her and leaned over the edge of the balcony. "Fine. You know what you have to do then."

"We don't know how they'll react to this. There's still hope," said Anael. "For once, it wouldn't hurt you to have a little—"

"If you say the F-word, I swear I will set you on fire," said Lucifer.

"Fine, be that way." Anael's wings extended. "We always knew this would be a possibility, Lucifer. In spite of everything, I still respect you and I wish I could have seen this through. But I am now and have always been an angel first. And you've always known that."

"Oh yes, I certainly remember," he said.

Anael narrowed her eyes. "Fine, play the role of the petulant child. You certainly wear it well." Her wings wrapped around her and in a flash of blue light, she was gone.

Lucifer emptied his drink in one gulp and then hurled the glass against the balcony's floor. It shattered. He leaned over the balcony again and stared out at the moon reflecting off the surface of the lake in the distance.

Without Anael, his chances of mounting an effective defense had just been drastically diminished. He had severe doubts as to whether or not he could handle the job on his own.

"My Lord?" asked Belial, emerging out onto the balcony. "I sensed an energy discharge. Is everything all right?"

"No, Belial, it's not," said Lucifer. "The outcome is no longer as sure as I'd thought."

"Where's Anael?"

"Gone. Summoned by the Choir," said Lucifer.

"What will you do now?"

Lucifer shook his head. "I haven't figured that part out yet."

CHAPTER 16

nael crossed the dimensional threshold into the outskirts of Heaven. A series of universes were all scattered against the black void, each one represented by a glowing orb, and they were all linked together by lines of energy flowing from one to another. All those universes eventually converged in a large orb at the center.

This was her destination—Elysium, the capital city of Heaven. Anael flew into the orb and once the brightness faded, she was surrounded by a soft, blue sky and clouds floating everywhere. Smooth, rounded spires made of crystal jutted forth from the clouds, with platforms scattered about. There was no indication of the ground or where the spires ended, they just faded into the clouds below.

Elysium was bustling as usual, with angels flying between the spires or conversing while perched on clouds or platforms. None greeted her as she flew past. Most wouldn't even look at her. And of the ones that did, the expressions on their face hardly conveyed friendly intent.

She supposed word had already spread about the trial. Uriel must have learned of it somehow—this whole thing stunk of his rumor-mongering. Seemed likely that's how the Choir learned of this as well.

Anael flew towards the largest spire in the center of Elysium. There was a platform with an opening that led into the structure. Anael landed here and she was glad to see at least one face that seemed friendly. Gabriel was waiting for her on the platform and he greeted her with a hug—albeit a very short and quick one.

"Welcome back, sister," he said.

"I wish I could say it's good to be back, but I don't think I'm going to like this, am I?"

Gabriel's jovial expression softened. "No, I'm afraid you won't."

"Can you give me some warning of what I've got to expect?"

"I can tell you that the Choir's not happy. They found out about the trial and your role."

"Uriel, I'm guessing?"

"Seems likely." Gabriel led Anael inside the structure. There was a large orb hovering in the middle of the otherwise-empty room. "They want answers, Anael. And a piece of advice—you want to be as honest with them as possible. Don't try to equivocate and definitely don't lie."

"I'll do my best," said Anael.

Both angels placed their hands upon the orb and closed their eyes. Gabriel spoke the prayer of request.

"This daughter of Heaven hath been summoned to an audience with the Divine Choir. We humbly beseech thee in the name of the Presence to be granted access to their holy temple."

"In the Presence's name, amen," added Anael.

The orb responded to the prayer by pulsating and the glow expanded until it engulfed the pair. Even behind her eyelids, Anael could see how bright it became. As the light faded, she opened her eyes and they stood in a vast expanse of clouds with a calming light. They were surrounded by angels who were haloed with light so bright, it obscured their features. It was impossible to see how many there were, but the one detail that was clear were the three pairs of wings each of the angels possessed.

"O mighty seraphim of the Divine Choir, the archangel Gabriel has fulfilled his duty and brought before you the one you seek," said Gabriel, kneeling before the Choir.

Anael got down on both knees and bent forward, holding her hands out in front of her head. "O Divine Choir, I am named Anael of the malakim. I am grateful for the honor to appear before you this day."

"Rise, malakim," said the Choir. They spoke all at once in a unified voice that sounded like a chorus. **"You may not be so grateful once this meeting has concluded."**

"Any opportunity to be in the presence of the Divine Choir is an opportunity to be grateful for, no matter the content," said Anael as she stood.

"The Presence has recently made us aware of a troubling development. The Adversary is being placed on trial by the denizens of Hell."

"Forgive my ignorance, O wise seraphim, but may I be enlightened as to why that's troubling?"

The key when speaking to the Divine Choir was reverence. Questions must always be couched in the language of pursuing knowledge. If they came off as interrogative, that would be seen as questioning the will of Heaven itself. The Choir, by and large, was not a fan of questions.

"It is not the trial the Presence objects to. What Hell does with its own is their business. The true question is one of your involvement. Exactly why would an angel

of the malakim—held in such high regard for her role in exposing subterfuge all those eons ago—provide aid and comfort to the Adversary?"

"May I speak freely in this realm, my Lords?" asked Anael.

"You may."

"Heaven is a place of law and order. We angels pride ourselves on our civility. We have structures and systems in place to deal with conflicts. We do not resolve our differences through barbarism. And so I felt a trial of the Adversary would be the perfect such venue."

"While your argument has a ring of truth to it, it does not explain your involvement."

"The law must be impartial, my Lords. And that means that every being, no matter how reprehensible their crimes, must be given a fair defense."

The temple was heavy with silence. The lights of the seraphim pulsated in different patterns, perhaps signifying some form of communication amongst them. No one really knew how the seraphim deliberated these matters. Anael glanced at Gabriel, but his expression conveyed a similar lack of knowledge. Neither could tell where this meeting would proceed next.

"Your argument is not without merit, Anael of the malakim. However, should any angel serve as counsel to the Adversary—or for that matter, any denizen of Hell—it would be misconstrued as an endorsement of their actions by the power of Heaven. And this is something the Presence cannot permit."

"May I ask how the Adversary will defend himself in this trial?" asked Anael.

"That is not our concern. The Desolate One placed

himself in this position, and so the consequences are his alone to bear."

Anael sighed. It was the expected outcome, but it didn't change the fact that she was disappointed. There was more to be known, however. "If the Divine Choir permits it, may I ask a question?"

There was a brief silence as the seraphim's lights pulsated between each other. Another signal of their silent communication. **"Proceed."**

"When Lu—when the Adversary first approached me about serving in his defense, we were attacked by the warden of Gehenna. I was wondering why he was sent after us?"

"Kushiel's mission is of no concern to you, Anael of the malakim. He is a servant of Heaven and that is all you need to know."

"May I inquire as to my next assignment?" asked Anael. "Since Uriel dismissed me from his service, I have had no task."

"Nor shall you receive one any time soon. For the time being, you are ordered to remain within the celestial city of Elysium. You must not under any circumstances travel to any other realms. Is that understood, Anael of the malakim?"

Anael gave a solemn nod. "Yes, my Lords. I understand and shall comply with your commands."

"Consider this a form of penance, Anael of the malakim. Should you prove yourself worthy of our trust once more, then you shall be rewarded with a new task. Until such time as we deem it so, you are dismissed."

The light from the seraphim expanded and became blindingly bright. It faded almost as quickly and both

Anael and Gabriel were back standing by the orb, its glow dimming.

"I'm sorry, Anael." Gabriel placed a hand on her back and led her out to the open-air platform. "If it's any consolation, the Choir gave me a similar sentence after my involvement in the Pyriel affair. Just keep your head down and it will all blow over soon."

"Did you notice something odd about that meeting, Gabriel?" she asked.

Gabriel cocked an eyebrow. "Odd? I'm not sure I understand what you mean."

"Before we went into the temple, you seemed pretty confident that Uriel was how the Choir learned about the trial. But they said it was the Presence."

"Seems I was wrong," said Gabriel with a shrug. "Of course it stands to reason that the Presence's omniscience would be aware of what was happening in Hell."

"His omniscience…of course…" said Anael.

Gabriel gave her a quizzical look. "Is it just me or does it seem like you've got something on your mind?"

Anael just shook her head and gave him a smile. "No, it's nothing. I suppose I'm just a little tired after everything that's happened. If you don't mind, I think I'd like to return to my quarters and get some rest."

"Of course," said Gabriel. "And don't worry about Lucifer. I'm certain he'll find some way to pull through this. The Morningstar is nothing if not resourceful."

"You're right. Goodbye, Gabriel. I'll talk to you later."

Anael launched herself from the platform and flew through the city. She had to remain here, that she would abide by. But she had no intention of simply confining herself to her room. There were questions Anael wanted answered and the only way she would find those answers was by first doing some research. She felt the need to catch up on some history.

CHAPTER 17

The courtroom was uncharacteristically silent as everyone waited for the second phase of the trial to begin. Lucifer sat alone at the defense table and would occasionally glance back towards the door. He hadn't heard from Anael since she left to meet with the Choir, and that only seemed to confirm his suspicions—they'd ordered her to drop the case and as the good little soldier she was, she wouldn't violate their command.

Asmodeus stood to address the court. "Well, I believe we've waited long enough. Are we going to proceed with this or not?"

"Guess that's up to the defendant," said Baron Samedi, casting a furtive glance in Lucifer's direction. "What say you, boy? Seems pretty obvious your lawyer ain't comin' back. So you got two choices—you find someone else to represent you in the next ten seconds, or you forfeit the case an' we move right to sentencing."

Lucifer rose to his feet. He'd always served as his own advocate in all matters, so why should this time be any different? It would certainly be a challenge, but if his only other option was to lie down and give up, he wasn't prepared to go down that route.

"If it pleases the court, I'll be representing myself from this point on."

"I would like to issue an objection to that," said Asmodeus. "He can't just change counselors mid-trial."

"An' why not?" asked Samedi. "Where in the rules is any of this written?"

Asmodeus didn't have an answer.

"You go on, Morningstar. Call your first witness," said Samedi.

"I would like to call the King of Hell to the stand," said Lucifer.

All eyes turned to the box where the members of the Infernal Court sat. Luther Cross stood and moved past his fellow Hell Lords. He and Asmodeus exchanged angered glances as he walked by on his way to the witness box. Once Cross settled in, Lucifer began the questioning.

"State your parentage for the court," said Lucifer.

"My mother was Grace Cross, a human who was kidnapped and forced to bring a child to bear by a cult that worshipped my father," said Cross. "And my father was Abraxas, one of The Fallen."

"So you're a cambion—half-man, half-demon," said Lucifer.

Cross nodded.

"And you haven't died, correct?"

"I did, actually," said Cross. "But I got better."

Lucifer smirked. "But you became a Hell Lord prior to that, right?"

"Yeah," said Cross. "It's a long story, but I was able to get a position on the Court because of who my father was."

"Do you recall when you and I made a deal?"

"In exchange for helping me defeat Asmodeus, you

wanted something in return. At first you didn't say what it was. But later, you came clean and said you wanted me to take your place as the ruler of Hell."

"And what else did I tell you at that time?"

"You told me what you learned a long time ago," said Cross. "That the Presence was just a lie the Divine Choir used to keep people in check."

"Did I tell you why I had kept this secret?"

"Because you feared how angels would react. They were created to be servants, but knowing that there was nothing to serve could cause them to snap."

"And was my fear a reasonable one or not? Did anything happen to justify this concern?"

"There was another angel who discovered the truth. Real bastard by the name of Pyriel. And he went nuttier than a Mr. Peanuts factory," said Cross. "He even tried to start the apocalypse all by his lonesome because of what he'd learned."

"So my concern was all rooted in a desire to keep the people of Hell safe, correct?"

"That's the sense I got," said Cross.

"Thank you, Lord Cross. No further questions at this time."

Before Lucifer had even returned to his seat, Asmodeus had already stood and was approaching the witness box.

"Were you raised by your parents, Cross?" asked Asmodeus.

Cross smirked right before he answered. "Actually, that's *Lord* Cross to you, *Mr.* Asmodeus."

The demon's face twitched at the jab but he covered it up with a forced smile of his own. He put on a show of apologizing dramatically. "So dreadfully sorry, your majesty. *Lord* Cross, were you raised by your parents?"

"No," said Cross. "My mother died during childbirth. Shortly after, I was rescued from my father's cult by a man named Alistair Carraway."

"And so this Carraway raised you himself?"

"No, he was part of an organization. That's where I grew up."

"An organization called the Sons of Solomon, correct?"

Cross nodded. "Yes."

"Now, correct me if I'm wrong, Lord Cross, but don't the Sons of Solomon *hunt* demons?" asked Asmodeus.

"Among other things, yes," said Cross.

"So before becoming a Hell Lord, you were a demon hunter?"

"I prefer the term 'paranormal investigator.'"

"Did you or did you not kill demons in the course of your duties?" asked Asmodeus.

"I killed demons who—"

"Thank you, Lord Cross."

He wasn't finished trying to answer, despite Asmodeus speaking over him. Luther tried to raise his voice to get his full explanation in. "Demons who violated the rules of Hell and whose only purpose—"

"Your Dishonor, I believe the witness has completed his answer," said Asmodeus.

Samedi banged the gavel. "Yeah, I concur with that. The witness can keep silent until asked another question."

Cross's eyes burned bright scarlet in response to the judge's admonishment as Asmodeus continued speaking to the jury.

"I'd like to draw attention to a very significant fact

raised by this witness's testimony," said Asmodeus. "The defendant did not see fit to trust any demon in Hell with the knowledge of the Divine Choir's lies. And when it came time to select a successor, the Morningstar chose not one of his lieutenants, but instead chose a man whose life mission was destroying demons. Thank you."

Asmodeus returned to his seat, but Lucifer stood. He wasn't going to let Asmodeus leave it on that note.

"If I may ask one rebuttal question, your Dishonor?" asked Lucifer.

Samedi rolled his eyes. "Fine, but make it quick."

"Lord Cross," Lucifer began, "In your time as a so-called 'demon hunter,' did you ever encounter a demon named Asmodeus?"

"Many times."

"And what kind of relationship did you share?"

"He was a source. I often went to him for information on what was happening in Chicago's supernatural under-world," said Cross. "He even saved my life once or twice."

Lucifer smirked and then gave a bow not unlike the showy types that characterized Asmodeus's questioning. "Thank you, Lord Cross. I have no further questions for you."

"Step down," said Samedi to Cross.

Luther descended from the witness box. As he walked past Asmodeus, he flashed his middle finger. Asmodeus returned the gesture in kind. Lucifer ignored the petty exchange between the two enemies and remained standing to call his next witness.

"At this time, your Dishonor, the defense would like to call the Morningstar to the stand."

"You gonna call yourself to testify?" asked Samedi.

"Why not?" Lucifer pointed at Asmodeus. "He did it."

"Sure, let's go ahead an' see how this plays out." Samedi banged the gavel.

Lucifer walked over to the witness box and stepped inside. He sat in the chair and addressed the jury.

"Did I intend to start a war with Heaven?" he began by asking himself the question. "No, I did not. My goal was never war. I never wanted to establish myself as any sort of king. But I was forced into that position by circumstance. I never wanted conflict with the Divine Choir, nor did I want to be subservient to them. All I ever wanted was for people to be permitted to pursue free will.

"Was I foolish to expect that to happen? Yes, I fully acknowledge that. I was embarrassingly naïve." Lucifer paused to take a breath. "For centuries, I served as the ruler of Hell because I felt there were too many on the Infernal Court who hungered for vengeance on Heaven. But I knew if there were to be a second war, there wouldn't be any winners. It would be a conflict so disastrous, it might consume the universe as a whole. I had no desire to see that happen. And so, I remained on the throne. For a long, *long* time.

"Did I build Cocytus as a way to appease the Choir? Yes, but it wasn't because I sought their approval. It was because I wanted to avert the potential for war," he continued. "During the incident with the angel Pyriel, I came to realize that perhaps my way wasn't working so well. I selected Cross not because of his past as a demon hunter, but because he was a child of all three worlds. He was born of a demon and a human, but raised in the ways of Heaven. I felt sincerely that he could be a bridge to those three worlds and hopefully improve things for the better.

"Do I wish I had done things differently? Of course.

I'm guiltier than anyone of the sins of vanity and pride. I put myself on trial so the people of Hell can have a saying of their own for once," said Lucifer. "Those are all the questions I have. If Asmodeus would like to question me, now he can feel free to do so."

"Gladly." Asmodeus stood and moved into the center of the court. "When you left Hell, what happened to Cocytus?"

"Without my presence in Hell, the magicks I used to forge Cocytus weakened."

"And that led to several of the inmates escaping, did it not?" asked Asmodeus.

"I'm sorry to say it did."

"So you were so concerned about preventing those inmates from starting a new war, that you allowed their prison to crack open? All so you could enjoy a retirement of leisure and debauchery?"

"That's an oversimplification," said Lucifer. "I had no idea at the time—"

"Let the record reflect that the defendant only cared about preventing war so long as it didn't inconvenience his own personal life," said Asmodeus. "These are not the actions of a hero, my friends. These are the actions of a selfish, arrogant child who put his own desires above the needs of everyone else."

"This coming from the demon who whored himself out to Purgatory—"

"And what of your wings, *Adversary*?" asked Asmodeus, emphasizing the last word. "The rest of The Fallen have all been transformed by Hell. But not you. Your angelic wings remained as pristine as ever, didn't they?"

"Yes, they did. In truth, I don't know why," said Lucifer. "I've always suspected it was a taunt by the Choir to remind me of what I'd lost."

"'Of what you lost,'" said Asmodeus with a huff. "I thought the whole point of rebelling from Heaven was that we'd be rising to something greater?"

"I never said I agreed with the Choir's belief, just the reason why they left my wings intact."

"Or it could mean that your wings remained because you've never left Heaven's service."

The last comment stung. Lucifer had also suspected that in recent time. In becoming the Devil the Choir made him out to be, he had in fact been doing their will.

"The prosecution has no further questions for this witness, your Dishonor," said Asmodeus, not allowing Lucifer an opportunity to answer the final taunt.

CHAPTER 18

During her meeting with the Choir, a thought occurred to Anael. The Presence was supposed to be omniscient, that's what the Choir had long taught every angel in Heaven. And yet, the Presence only commanded the Choir to take action on her participation in the trial once Uriel had learned of it.

The timing was very convenient and it made Anael wonder about other events. If the Presence was omniscient, shouldn't he have been able to predict Lucifer's actions all those centuries ago? Why wouldn't he act in advance to stop it instead of only playing catch-up? Why allow the rebellion and the war to proceed as it had, which led to the deaths of an untold number of angels on both sides of the conflict? And shouldn't he have been able to know about Lucifer's eventual abdication and Anael's decision to represent him in the trial?

It certainly wasn't about making choices for themselves. The Divine Choir had held ever since creation that free will was a lie. That chaos would reign supreme without the order they provided. This was supposed to be the will of the Presence himself and to question it was blasphemy.

Anael now realized those questions had always been in

the back of her mind, but only now did she acknowledge them. For the longest time, she just dismissed them. She wondered how many other angels had those same thoughts but similarly kept them hidden.

Anael sought clarification in the records of Heaven. Since she parted from Gabriel, she'd immersed herself in Elysium's massive library. The shelves extended all the way down into the clouds, with large archways separating each section of the library. Every book in here dealt with the nature of the Presence, Heaven, and the history of the universe. No books from any other realm, be it Earth, Hell, Purgatory or anywhere else, were permitted in this library.

It made for a dry reading experience, she now realized. These books weren't meant to entertain or even really to inform. They were very matter-of-fact in their presentation, with no sense of poetry or artistry in their prose. Reading these books was akin to reading an instruction manual. Worse, actually—instructions were clear, these records were not.

Anael had researched every calamity ever recorded. The Fall, the Nephilim Crisis, Abraxas's Rebellion, the Crucifixion of the Nazarene, all the great wars and plagues throughout human history. All the way up to Pyriel's attempt to start the apocalypse. Anael reviewed every single one of them.

Not once was there any mention of the Presence ever taking any action in advance to prevent these disasters. Nor was there a mention of the Presence having averted a crisis before it happened. Everything was always in reaction to these events.

Anael reviewed the authorship of the records. Only the earliest volumes of Heaven, those that were written long before The Fall, were transcribed by the Metatron. She recalled how Lucifer claimed to have learned the truth from Heaven's Scribe and how he had been hiding in Purgatory all this time. Perhaps, if Anael could locate Metatron, he would be able to provide some context for Lucifer's testimony. Help prove his cause.

"What are you doing?" she whispered to herself and sighed.

If she continued down this path, the Choir had made it clear that she'd be committing heresy. Was she prepared to take that risk of them finding out? And what if she was wrong and the Presence knew what she was up to, even now?

She wouldn't find those answers in Heaven. But there was one being in all of creation who could perhaps give her some guidance. A being older than Heaven itself. Reaching him would be a massive feat in its own right, though. And to find him, she'd have to go through some unorthodox means.

Anael left the library. The Choir forbade her from leaving Heaven, but the person she needed to speak to could be found on the very edge. All she needed was the currency to summon him. And to do that, she'd need help.

The vast majority of Earth's inhabitants were unaware of realms beyond their own and as such, travel to and from there was largely unrestricted. But when it came to other realms, the only way for outsiders to enter was through the River Styx. It wasn't a physical river, but a path that connected the disparate worlds together. Travel through the Styx required summoning Charon the Ferryman. But to summon him, one first needed the coins that Charon accepted as his sole payment.

In Heaven, the coins had to be requisitioned. Everything in Elysium was governed by structure and order, with matters too unimportant for the Choir to handle delegated to others. That meant there was a bureaucracy in place.

Once Anael left the library, she went to the spire housing the Temple of Pan-Dimensional Access. This was where angels came when they needed to travel to a non-Earth realm, with the Ferryman's coins requisitioned by an angel named Nathaniel.

Anael touched down on the platform and entered the temple. The place looked like the waiting room at the DMV with a number of windows for attendants. Only one of them was actually open, and that's where she saw Nathaniel.

Most angels were the models of physical perfection, but that wasn't the case with some of the lesser choirs. Nathaniel was one of these—he had a stocky frame and was dressed in a short-sleeved button-down shirt and slacks. Looking every bit like a typical public servant.

"Can I help you?" he asked.

"Yes, I'm here to claim the coins for summoning Charon," said Anael.

"Name?" he asked.

"Anael."

Nathaniel pulled open a drawer on his desk and flipped through the files out of Anael's view. "Let's see here…Adriel…Amitiel…Amnayel…Amriel…Anaphiel…" He shook his head. "I don't seem to have a record for Anael."

"Are you sure about that?" she asked.

"Quite sure. Have you spoken with your missionary leader? They were supposed to submit a Request for Access form and only once it's approved could you come here for your coins."

Anael feigned worry. "This isn't good...I was supposed to travel to Purgatory today."

"I'm sorry, but I can't help you."

"You don't understand..." Anael leaned forward over the separator and spoke in a whispered voice. "The Choir has personally ordered me to travel to Purgatory on a covert diplomatic mission."

"Covert? For what purpose?" asked Nathaniel.

Anael kept herself from smiling. Nathaniel was simple middle-management bureaucracy. He had no doubt never even left Elysium. To call his existence mundane would no doubt be generous.

"You've heard the latest rumors about the Adversary, right?"

"The...the Adversary?" asked Nathaniel. "What rumors?"

"You mean you *don't* know?"

"I...I don't *think* so..."

"Well, they're all true," said Anael. "The Morningstar has been put on trial by Hell. And Purgatory is acting as a neutral arbiter. The Choir has ordered me to speak with them regarding terms for the Adversary's eventual sentencing."

"Then why not file an official request?" asked Nathaniel.

"Maybe it's because the Choir can't be seen to be taking sides. Even me telling you this is risking the mission." Anael sighed.

"I wish I could help, but..."

Anael shook her head and started to turn away. "No, I'm sorry. You're right, I should go back to the Choir and tell them that Nathaniel requires an official request form. I just hope timing won't be an issue on this…"

"T-timing?" asked Nathaniel.

"Oh yes, you know how they are when it comes to ensuring things happen according to a specific schedule," said Anael. "I hope the delay won't have any knock-down effects. But if that's the case, I'm sure they'd understand that you were just following the rules."

Anael turned away from the window and proceeded to the exit. She barely made it a few steps before Nathaniel called out to her.

"Miss Anael, please wait a moment," he said.

Anael turned and went back to the window. "Yes? If I take too long to get back to the Choir, they may not be happy."

"Given the urgency of these circumstances and the…" he looked back and forth before whispering, "…secrecy of this mission, I *can* grant you an emergency use authorization. However, you will have to provide those requests after the fact."

"Of course, of course," said Anael. "You have no idea how wonderful this is of you. I'm sure the Choir will reward your dedication to our holy mission."

"Yes, please remind the Choir just how helpful I was, I'm sure they would love to hear that." Nathaniel slid a coin across the counter and Anael picked it up.

"Thank you again, Nathaniel. May the Presence be with you."

"And you," he said.

Anael left with the coin, though she had a sinking feeling in her stomach. She'd never used that kind of duplicity before and she wasn't sure how she felt about it. Lucifer would no doubt have found it endearing, but between helping him, breaking the Choir's commandments, and now this, Anael wondered just how close she was to falling herself.

CHAPTER 19

There was some surprise in the court when Lucifer stood and announced that he had no further witnesses to call. As he sat back down, he knew that Belial and Mara and more than likely some other of his fierce supporters would be left asking the question of why. Anael had planned to call at least some of them.

But this wasn't Anael's show anymore. Lucifer knew that the jury's minds had already been made up—in fact, they had probably settled on a verdict before the trial even began. Putting up loyalists who would testify to Lucifer's greatness might be good for his ego, but it wouldn't sway anyone on the fence.

The final statements were where the soundest arguments would be made. And if he were being honest with himself, Lucifer just wanted the whole kangaroo court to be over. He was tired and no matter the outcome, he just wanted to be finished with all of it.

"Since the defense rests, we'll move on to the final statements. Asmodeus, floor's all yours, boy," said Samedi.

Asmodeus stood and moved into the center of the courtroom to address the jury and everyone else gathered.

"Members of the jury, your Dishonor, the Infernal

Court. We have endured this trial for one purpose and one purpose alone—to judge the fate of the Morningstar and decide whether or not he should be held accountable for the crime of treason against the people of Hell," said Asmodeus. "Throughout this trial, I have demonstrated in painstaking detail just how the Morningstar put the desires of Heaven above the needs of Hell.

"You've heard in this trial how time and time again, Lucifer had betrayed his own fellows so that he could curry favor with the Divine Choir. Testimony not only from yours truly but also the Hell Lords Lilith and Beelzebub corroborate this fact. And if more proof is needed, the prosecution *would* have called the likes of Astaroth and Barbatos as well, but that wasn't really an option. Lucifer didn't leave much to question after he was done with them.

"You've heard how time and time again, he sought the favor of his angel lover. Not even in the face of her numerous betrayals did he ever hold it against her. No, he continued pining for her after all she'd done to him.

"The Morningstar had knowledge of the greatest lie ever perpetuated on the universe. And he kept the truth hidden to all but himself, thereby doing the will of the Choir. When he finally decided to reveal the truth—when he picked a successor—the one he chose wasn't one who had been loyal to him and Hell. No, he picked a half-breed who made a career out of *hunting* our kind!

"And then, you heard from the Morningstar himself. You heard him admit on the stand that it was his own abdication that cracked open the walls of Cocytus. He only cared about maintaining the peace so long as it didn't inconvenience his decadent lifestyle.

"The Morningstar is not like us. Everyone in Hell—

with some exceptions—" he shot a glare at Cross when he said that, "—was once something else. Human, angel, whatever. But when we came to Hell, we all were transformed by this glorious place—we became demons. And that ascension is a symbol, a giant 'fuck you' to the Choir and their 'plans' for us.

"But not Lucifer. No, the Morningstar's wings remained just as beautiful as they were in Heaven. If not for his eyes, you'd be forgiven if you mistook him for an angel. He still looks like one of them." Asmodeus moved closer to the jury, staring each of the members in the eye. "That's because he still *is* one of them. He's never ceased being their whore, their dutiful little errand boy.

"If Hell is going to truly cast off the shackles of Heaven, then we must take the first step by declaring our independence from the Morningstar and all he represents. We must forge a new destiny for all of demonkind. And for that to happen, you must find the defendant guilty on all counts. Thank you."

Asmodeus ended his statement with another bow and then returned to his seat. Samedi turned his attention over to Lucifer. "You sure you wanna go after all that, boy?"

"Absolutely."

Lucifer rose to his feet and stepped into the center. He took a deep breath and as he exhaled, his wings emerged from his back in a showy display of his plumage. He met the eyes of everyone in the courtroom before he spoke.

"I can tell these wings make you all nervous. In your mind, they remind you of the enemy. Those who expelled us from paradise and remain a continuing existential threat. But that's not what these wings remind me of. Nor do they indicate my loyalties, as Asmodeus would want you to believe," he said. "Instead, they remind me of missed opportunities and past mistakes.

"Yes, I maintained the Divine Choir's lie. When I learned the truth, I wanted to broadcast it all across Elysium. But in the back of my head, I had doubts. Part of me didn't want to believe what I'd learned. Like all the other angels, I had devoted my existence to serving the Presence, and to discover that I'd promised myself to a lie was difficult to process. I needed to hear from another before I could do anything.

"I trusted Anael more than any other angel in Heaven. If she believed me, then I knew there was the possibility that other angels would, too. But when she rejected my words as some sort of madness, I knew how the rest of Heaven would react. The purpose of angels was to serve, no different from bees or ants serving the needs of their queen. At least that's what they believed.

"I felt that like me, all angels had the potential for more, if only the circumstances were right. If I showed them what free will looked like, I felt they would eventually come around. And so, I worked an ancient spell to awaken the spark within mankind. To show the angels what they could aspire to.

"It didn't work the way I'd hoped. And from the moment we landed in Hell, I knew that these souls were now my responsibility. I had to do whatever I could to maintain their safety and security.

"It didn't help when many of the newly-created demons dedicated their lives to vengeance on Heaven. Yes, I appeased the Choir when they made demands upon me. I did this because the firepower of Heaven was far greater than what we in Hell had. There was simply no other choice.

"Eventually, I grew tired. The revolution wasn't just over, it had never really happened. I felt Hell needed new leadership, but it couldn't be anyone obsessed with the past. We needed to look to a new future and I would retire.

"My plan backfired. I hadn't counted on Cocytus cracking open and the sins of my past coming back to haunt me.

"So yes, I concede that I've made my fair share of mistakes. But Asmodeus's accusation is just false. I did what I did not because I was following the orders of the Divine Choir or anyone else. The mistakes I made, I made them because I am fallible. Just like every single being in this room today. Just like everyone on Earth, in Purgatory, in every single realm in the universe—including Heaven.

"Perfection is a lie. An unattainable goal we nonetheless must continue to strive for."

Lucifer retracted his wings and bowed his head.

"My fate is in the hands of this jury. Should you choose to convict me of the treason Asmodeus has accused me of, then I'll accept that judgment. But know that you're simply perpetuating the same cycles that brought us to this point. And you will *not* stop the Divine Choir's machinations by punishing me.

"Just before this trial, the Choir sent Heaven's jailer after me. He was stopped only because he learned that this trial was happening. I have no doubt that was just a temporary stay and that the Choir isn't finished involving themselves here.

"But if you allow people like Asmodeus to win, they will escalate. They will make the situation far worse. I'm not saying that I'm the answer—clearly, I'm not. That's why I stepped down in the first place. But what I am saying is that neither are those calling for more blood.

"Thank you."

Lucifer returned to his seat. Silence hung in the courtroom for a long while. All eyes turned to the judge. Baron Samedi sat in his chair with his eyes cast downwards, apparently deep in thought. After a few moments, a snore was heard.

The Morningstar sighed. This whole thing had been one big joke. All an excuse for theatre. Once the verdict came down, Samedi would want his prize. Assuming, of course, the Choir didn't get involved in some way.

The judge stirred awake. "Sorry, is it over? Okay, jurors, you get some time to decide what we gonna do with the defendant." Samedi banged the gavel and court was adjourned so the jury could begin their deliberation.

CHAPTER 20

On the outskirts of Elysium was where the Styx met the Celestial City. Long ago, Lucifer had come here to summon the Ferryman on his own path to enlightenment. Anael knew because he'd told her the story. She never imagined that she would one day do the same.

She stared at the coin used to summon the Ferryman, turning it over and over in her hand, debating yet again whether or not she was making the right choice. It wasn't too late. She could simply turn back now, return the coin to Nathaniel, and leave it at that. If the Choir ever learned anything, she could explain it away as a temporary bout of insanity, brought on by a prolonged stay on Earth in the proximity of the Adversary. No doubt they would certainly accept that as an excuse.

Try as she might, she couldn't quite bring herself to turn away. She just stared at the coin, turning it as it reflected the celestial light above. This had the potential to change her life in ways she couldn't yet comprehend.

Anael closed her eyes and—with a silent prayer to a god she was no longer certain even existed—tossed the coin into the river. It sank quickly beneath the surface.

The banks were silent. And then, gradually the fog that

hung over the Styx in the distance rolled closer. Anael tried to stare into the opaque wisps and in the midst, she could see one single light. A long boat moved into view, a lantern hanging at the stern. Standing at the back and rowing the boat with a long oar was a slim figure in a heavy robe. Strands of white hair poked out the sides of his hood and his eyes glowed within the darkness.

He brought the boat to a stop parallel to the shore and stared out at the angel. With a finger, he beckoned her forth. Anael's wings raised her from the ground and brought her closer to the boat. Before she could set foot in the vessel, he held up his hand in a gesture to halt her.

"Why have you summoned me, angel?" he asked.

"I need to speak with Death."

She couldn't see Charon's face within the darkness of his hood, so she had no idea how he'd reacted to the statement. He remained silent for a few moments, just the steady glow of his eyes as the only sign that he was even still alive.

"Death doesn't take visitors," he simply said.

"Once long ago, you took the Morningstar on an unsanctioned journey to learn the truth, to find the Metatron," said Anael. "Why would you even have done something like that?"

"My reasons are my own," said the Ferryman. "I answer to neither Heaven nor Hell."

"No, you only answer to one being in all of creation. You're the only connection we have to him," said Anael. "He was the one who sent you back then, wasn't he?"

"You do not know what you ask of me. To grant you an audience with my master without his express invitation would be heresy of the highest order."

"Then what was the purpose of showing the Morningstar the truth?" asked Anael. "Just so he could end up a prisoner of Heaven?"

Charon flinched at that. "Of what do you speak?"

"The Divine Choir sent their jailer after Lucifer. I don't know what exactly they're planning, but I'm certain it's contrary to anything your master wants to happen," said Anael.

Silence again hung in the air, just as heavy as the fog that surrounded them. Anael felt that at any moment, the Ferryman would simply roll back into the distance without another word.

"If you do this, there is something you must understand," said Charon. "My master is more powerful than all the angels in Heaven. Should he have no desire to entertain your presence, he can and will easily scatter your atoms across the universe."

Anael swallowed, but nodded. "Yes, I'm aware of how powerful he is."

"Is this a risk you're willing to take?"

"Not really, no. But I'm otherwise out of options."

"Very well." Charon pointed to an empty spot in the boat. "My vessel is yours for now."

Anael bowed her head in thanks and flew over the boat. She gently set herself inside and sat on the bench.

"Please be mindful of your surroundings. And whatever you do, don't fall over the edge," he warned. "Not even an angel could escape the Styx."

The Styx existed in a kind of void that separated the different realms. A dense fog hung over them during the entire journey. Anael wondered exactly how Charon was able to navigate this strange path. Time itself felt like an abstract concept in this place, even more so than it did in Heaven.

Beams of light slowly began to pierce the veil. The vapor was thinner as they continued forward. The fog completely broke finally, and Anael closed her eyes at the sudden brightness that fell on her face.

They were no longer in some ethereal void, but now on what looked like an ocean navigating towards a sandy beach. Charon would only take her in so far and at a certain point, he brought the boat to a stop.

"This is as far as I go," he said. "From this moment on, you will be on your own. It will be your duty to explain to my master why you have come to see him. Should he accept your petition, he shall grant you an audience. But should he not—"

"My atoms will be scattered across the universe," said Anael, repeating Charon's own words. "I remember."

"Should you survive…" Charon produced a coin from the sleeve of his robe and held it out, "…you may summon me again to return you to Heaven."

"Assuming I'm still welcome there." Anael took the coin from the Ferryman. "Thank you for doing this."

"Hold off on any expressions of gratitude," said Charon. "They may prove immature."

Anael nodded. She flew from the boat and her wings carried her the distance across the water until she reached the shoreline. Gently, Anael's feet touched down on the sand and she started walking.

The beach stretched endlessly into the horizon. Only one structure was found in the expanse of sand, and that was a small house with a pier that extended onto the water. There was a set of stairs leading up to the pier and just beside the staircase was a white motorcycle.

Anael climbed the steps and walked over to the door. There was a mat that read, "IMMORTALITY: A FATE WORSE THAN DEATH." She raised her fist, but hesitated before knocking. She'd finally gotten here, but she wasn't sure what she was going to say. And Charon's warning still stayed with her.

She took a breath and rapped her knuckles on the wooden surface. Every moment that she had to wait until the door opened felt like an eternity. It got to be so long that Anael wondered if she should knock again, or would that simply risk his anger?

When the door opened, Anael realized that she hadn't known what to expect when she came face to face with Death. But whatever it was she thought he would look like, she certainly didn't expect a man with short, silver hair and horn-rimmed glasses dressed in a black polo shirt and khakis. But that's what she got.

"Well, this is a...uh...interesting surprise," he said. "I certainly wasn't expecting any visitors today. Or any day, really. But since you're already here, I suppose I should hear what you have to say."

"You're...Death?" she asked.

"Why, were you expecting someone else?"

Anael shook her head.

"Good, because that would've been a little awkward. You coming to my house but not looking for me. Seems like a weird situation, doesn't it?" Death opened the door and gestured inside the house. "Sorry, where are my manners? Here I am droning on and I haven't even invited you in yet."

Anael nodded her thanks and carefully stepped inside the house. The living room was nicely furnished and even had a good balance of color in it. A large bookcase was up against one wall, the shelves filled to capacity. There were various potted plants and flowers all around, which felt strange to her.

"I know, the plant thing seems strange. But when you're…well…me, everything about your existence has to do with death," he said. "So I like to surround myself with life as much as possible. Now please, sit, sit."

Anael retracted her wings and sat in a white leather recliner. Death laid down across a couch and put his hands under his head.

"So you are Anael, right?"

"I am, yes," she said. "The reason I'm here is because—"

"Because you want something from me, of course." Death sighed. "Y'know, how come nobody ever comes by to just hang out? I'm a pretty fun guy. And I make one hell of a margarita and I've got this killer beachfront property. Instead it's always, 'Oh Death, I really need these people slaughtered' or 'Death, can you help me resurrect this person who really shouldn't have died?' or 'I don't want to die, how about we play a game for the fate of my soul?'"

"I'm sorry?" said Anael. "I was given the impression that you don't really like visitors."

Death sat up on the couch. "And where did you get that idea? Who doesn't like companionship?" He scoffed. "Wait, Charon, right? I get the guy means well, but he's a little too overprotective of my personal space. Won't even set foot on the beach himself. Is it because I'm too intimidating?"

"Well…you *are* Death."

"Good point," he said. "Okay, what is it *you* want from me?"

"It's about the Morningstar," she said.

Death rubbed his hands together and gave a knowing nod as he said, "Ahh yes. What a disappointment he turned out to be."

Anael cocked her head to the side. "What do you mean by that?"

"A long time ago, I arranged for him to receive the knowledge he needed to upend everything. But he just sat on it," said Death. "I thought of all the angels, he'd be the one best-suited to be a messenger of the truth. Instead, he did nothing with it except foment a useless rebellion."

Anael looked down, fumbling with her hands. "That… may have been my fault. Lucifer tried to reveal the truth to me. But I wasn't willing to listen. And because of that—"

"He felt *no* angel would listen," said Death. "I suppose I shouldn't be *too* harsh on him. Perhaps I wasn't clear enough when I had Charon lead him to the Scribe…"

"But there is something you can do now," said Anael. "The truth has gotten out. And Lucifer is on trial in Hell for conspiring with the Divine Choir."

"What?" asked Death. "That's the most ridiculous thing I've ever heard."

"That's why he needs your help," said Anael. "I need to find Metatron, to serve as a witness in the trial."

"Metatron can't really help you, my dear," said Death. "You see, after he revealed the truth to Lucifer, Metatron went into a kind of…uh…celestial witness protection program. Not even I know where he is and there's not a lot I don't know."

That sinking feeling Anael had felt before now returned. "So what can I do? I'm afraid that even if Lucifer is found innocent, the Choir has plans of their own. They already sent Kushiel to take him prisoner."

"That's certainly not what I'd expected…at least not at this date…"

"What do you mean by that?" asked Anael.

"You know of Metatron's prophecies?"

"Of course."

"In one of the prophecies, the Adversary is to be bound by the powers of Heaven. But that only occurs *after* several other events, including the coming of the Horsemen."

"You're talking about the Apocalypse?" asked Anael. "And aren't you one of the Horsemen?"

"That's exactly right, but I haven't been summoned. Nor have I heard anything from my siblings. There are many things Metatron's prophecies speak of which have yet to pass…" Death's eyes moved from side to side as he sat in thought. "Something's definitely not right here…"

"Then what can we do about it?" asked Anael.

"I have an idea, but there's no guarantee it will work," said Death. "And if you go down this route, you have to understand that there will be no going back."

"What is it?" asked Anael.

Death stood and walked over to the bookcase and ran his finger over the spines. Anael wondered how he knew which book was which, as none seemed to have any writing at all on the spines. Death selected a cyan-colored book and opened it up, flipping through the pages.

"Ah, here we are."

He reached his hand inside the book and pulled something out. Looking at Anael's direction, he tossed the object to her. She caught it and then examined it in her hand.

"Toss that into the Styx and Charon will take you where you need to go," said Death.

Anael looked at the coin. It had the number 8 stamped into the metal. But she realized there was a kind of dimensionality to the figure—it had two sides. And then she realized it wasn't an 8 at all, but actually seemed to be the symbol for infinity.

"Where does this coin lead to?"

"To maybe the only being in all creation who can help the Morningstar now," said Death.

CHAPTER 21

The verdict came quickly and court was called back into session. As he sat and pondered the fate chosen by a random grouping of demons selected from the different domains of Hell, Lucifer couldn't help but wonder if the haste was a good omen or bad.

Asmodeus certainly seemed sure of his chances. He sat at his table with a look of barely-restrained glee on his face. Like a child who knows Christmas morning is about to come. Was that just arrogance or did he know something the Morningstar didn't? Lucifer certainly wouldn't put it past the demon to have done some sort of backroom deal. He could almost bet on it.

"So, we ready to see how this ends?" asked Samedi, banging the gavel to bring the court to attention. He looked at the jury. "You figure out what's to be done with the Morningstar?"

The jury foreman stood to address the court. "We have, your Dishonor. On the charges of consorting and collaborating with the enemy, the jury finds the defendant…"

There was a pause in the foreman's reading of the verdict. A pause that felt like an eternity. Lucifer dreaded the next words out of the demon's mouth.

"…not guilty."

That feeling of dread was suddenly replace with a rush of excitement. He was free of this madness? Free of the Choir's attempted manipulations, free of the Infernal Court's backstabbing politics?

"However…" the foreman continued, "on the charge of treason against the denizens of Hell, the jury concludes that although there was no conscious effort on the part of the defendant to collaborate with the enemy, he nonetheless acted in a manner born out of self-interest. He prioritized his own concerns above those of Hell. And on that charge, the jury finds him guilty."

Lucifer did his best to remain stoic and avoid any appearance of disappointment. He was prepared for the worst. This wasn't an ideal ending, but it also wasn't as bad as it could have been. But what still disturbed him was the smile on Asmodeus's face. Only guilty on one count, and yet he still looked as if he had won total victory. Just what else was he planning?

"Now that we got that outta the way, I assume the prosecution has a sentencing request?" asked Samedi.

"Indeed I do." Asmodeus rose to his feet. "Your Dishonor, Hell no longer has a prison. The defendant saw to that when he destroyed Cocytus. And to have him be held in any of the realms of Hell would simply inflict more pain and suffering on those residents. The prosecution believes the only just punishment would be to remand the Morningstar to confinement in Limbo until such a time as it's determined by the Infernal Court that his sentence has been served."

Limbo was a realm of stillness. Unlike even Cocytus, it was a unique place where time and space truly had no meaning. Like remaining locked in a sensory-deprivation tank until you could find a method of escape.

"Does the defendant have any objection to the sentencing request?" asked Samedi.

"I do," said Lucifer, standing as well and shooting Asmodeus a glare. "Limbo is not a place for sentient beings. This is a punishment that simply shifts responsibility away from the Court."

"Yeah, it does do that," Samedi concurred, "but I kinda like it anyway. So I'm gonna let this happen."

Samedi banged his gavel and Lucifer wondered just what Asmodeus was plotting. Limbo seemed a strange choice. The entry points weren't as strictly controlled as those of most realms. Escape was far easier than it would be even in one of the territories of Hell. Something else was going on here, but in order to learn that, for the time Lucifer would have to go along with this.

"If that's all, then I'm gonna adjourn this court an' go back to my own concerns." Samedi banged the gavel one final time. When he did, his body suddenly exploded into about a dozen crows that all flew off.

Asmodeus turned his attention to Lucifer, that grin still on his face. "I hope you enjoy your new home. Should prove quite interesting to see what you do with the place."

"Don't think I can't smell your treachery, Asmodeus," said Lucifer. "I still remember you back when you were a snot-nosed little angel begging for favor. And I know when you've got a scheme brewing."

Asmodeus feigned a look of innocence. "Why, your words sting me, Lucifer. What could I possibly do to the likes of *you*?"

He chuckled as he walked out of court. Belial moved

past Asmodeus and approached his master.

"What now?" he asked.

"Now, I'm to be remanded to Limbo," said Lucifer.

"It won't stick. We'll find a way to free you sooner rather than later," said Belial.

"I know you will, and I also know Asmodeus is expecting that, too," said Lucifer. "Which makes me very suspicious."

They were interrupted by the approach of Grant and Moore.

"Very disappointing outcome in the trial, wouldn't you say so, Mr. Grant?"

"Quite an unexpected turn, Mr. Moore."

"And what do you both want?" asked Lucifer.

"Considering that Mr. Moore and I are neutral officers of the court, it shall be our duty to ferry you to your new home."

"Mr. Grant speaks the truth, Mr. Lucifer. We are to be your transportation to a wondrous new world."

"Not quite sure I'd use those exact words…" muttered Lucifer.

"He goes now?" asked Belial. "We have no opportunity to contest the outcome?"

"Pardon me, Mr. Grant, but would you inform me whether or not there is an appeals court in Hell?"

Grant shook his head. "I'm afraid I've never heard of such a thing, Mr. Moore. Ergo, it would seem there is no one left to hear such an appeal."

Lucifer approached his loyal follower and placed a hand on his shoulder. "Belial, it's fine. Thank you for all you've done. But this is how it must be now."

"This isn't over, my Lord," said Belial.

Lucifer nodded in understanding and then briefly tapped a finger to his lips, an indication for Belial to remain silent. He then turned to the two Purgatory operatives.

"Very well. If it has to be now, then we might as well get it over with."

Grant and Moore turned to each other in unison and joined together just as before for the briefest of moments to create a tear in time and space. Nothing could be seen on the other side of the portal whatsoever. Lucifer even tried briefly peering through only to find nothing. He gave one final look at Belial and then stepped inside the portal.

Where he found himself was a vast, black void, completely without substance. There was no sense of direction or dimensionality in this world and he had no way of knowing if he was alone or not. It was just as he expected Limbo to be—utterly and totally empty.

Lucifer tried testing his voice a few times by calling out. His own voice echoed back at him from all directions, even beneath him. This was Limbo, a total absence of everything. And this was where he was to spend however long the Infernal Court deemed his sentence should last.

"Well, well, *well*." The voice was a familiar one, accompanied by what sounded like the flapping of wings.

"So it seems I'm not as alone as I thought." Lucifer watched as a figure formed from the darkness and stepped forward.

Gone were the gown and powdered wig and he was back to wearing the top hat, though the skull face-paint and sunglasses remained.

"Nice of you to visit, Baron."

Samedi had an unsettling grin on his face. "So seems to

me we got some options here, Lucy ol' boy. You can stay in here and rot, or…"

"Or I can own up to our end of the bargain early, and give you my soul," said Lucifer.

Samedi held up a wagging finger. "Not just your soul, boy. But the power that comes with it. And then you can ride off into the sunset."

"The deal was for me to finish what needs doing," said Lucifer.

"Ain't you done that?" asked Samedi. "Your prison problem's been dealt with, and you don't gotta worry about Hell anymore. You in Limbo now, boy. How else you gonna get out?"

"Believe you me, Baron, I have a plan even for this," said Lucifer.

"'Cuz your plans got such a great track record, eh?"

"Our deal was you don't get my power until I'm done with it. And I'm not done with it yet," said Lucifer.

Samedi's eyes smoldered and his lips tightened, but somehow contained the visible anger on his face. "Fair does, Mr. Devil. Just don't be taking *too* long with that. There's only so much patience Baron Samedi possesses, and you've used up a good bit of it already."

He reached inside his jacket and Lucifer recoiled, prepared for an attack of some kind. Instead, all he did was produce a knife forged of bone, which he tossed in the Morningstar's direction. Lucifer caught it and examined the weapon. It was small, about the size of a pen knife.

"What am I supposed to do with this?" he asked.

The loa said nothing, just stepped back into the darkness and vanished as quickly as he appeared. Lucifer wondered whether Samedi knew that he'd completely lied when he said he had a plan for this. Belial could find a way to get him out of Limbo, but then there was the problem of how to stall Samedi even further, how Hell would respond once they learned he was free, and of course, the threat of Kushiel was still hanging over his head like the Sword of Damocles.

The walls were closing in. It wasn't just Samedi's patience that was at an end, so were the Morningstar's options.

CHAPTER 22

With the aid of Purgatory's agents, Asmodeus and Uriel once again met in the strange void between realities. Asmodeus practically had a spring in his step as he entered the void and took his seat. He leaned back in his chair and propped his feet on the table.

"Well, you certainly seem to be in good spirits," said Uriel, who sat down normally and folded his hands together on the table's surface. "I take it the trial went well?"

"Better than expected, in fact," said Asmodeus. "Seems you won't have to deal with the Infernal Court at all, not even through me. Lucifer's sentence has been carried out and now, he's just waiting for Kushiel to come claim him."

"And you're certain the Court isn't monitoring him?" asked Uriel with a hint of skepticism.

Asmodeus nodded. "Trust me, where he's been sent, monitoring is pretty much impossible. They couldn't keep tabs on him even if they wanted to, and my guess is most on the Court would just rather put this whole matter behind them. They're all selfish and short-sighted, more concerned with their own little realms than they are with the bigger picture. The only one who ever thought different was Abraxas."

"Yes, and we saw where that got him," said Uriel. "Very well, so tell me where he is."

"First, we've got some business to discuss," said Asmodeus. "I've lived up to my end of the bargain so far. How about yours?"

Uriel took a sharp intake of breath. He hated being ordered by a traitor like Asmodeus, but he only had to put up with the little demonic shit for a short time more.

"I spoke to the Choir about your…proposal," said Uriel. "In exchange for Lucifer, they're prepared to back your play for Hell's throne."

"And how do they plan to do that? Just saying they support me isn't enough, and probably wouldn't do my reputation much good."

"You know as well as I that the Choir can't just directly intervene in Hell's affairs. Such a move would be in direct violation of the armistice and thus reignite the war."

"There's got to be something you can do. I didn't go to all this trouble of setting the stage for nothing." Asmodeus took his feet off the table, then leaned forward and tapped the surface. "I want the thirty pieces of silver you promised me."

"You understand that this will be a long game," said Uriel. "We can have it arranged so that a member of the Court is eliminated. That will leave an opening which you, as one of The Fallen, will be a prime candidate for. Obviously we can't go directly after Cross, that will draw too much suspicion. But what about Lilith? That way, you can reclaim your former territory as well."

"My ex gets mysteriously taken out and I'm conveniently up for the territory she stole from me? Hitting Cross would be *less* suspicious than that," said Asmodeus. "No, it needs to be someone else. Preferably someone from the anti-Morningstar contingent of the Court. Then the attack can be blamed on one of Lucifer's followers and further damn his image in Hell."

"You know more about the personages of the Court and where they stand on the Morningstar question than I, so the decision is up to you," said Uriel.

"The choice is between Beelzebub, Nergal, Mammon, and Leviathan," said Asmodeus. "Leviathan is someone you don't want to mess with. She's as dangerous as they come. Nergal is a tough customer in his own right, though not to the same extent. Mammon might be the easiest to dispatch, but I think it obviously has to be Beelzebub."

"What makes it so obvious?" asked Uriel.

"What do you think?" asked Asmodeus. "Beelzebub already betrayed Lucifer by backing Raum. If he were to be killed and a Luciferian framed for the attack, it'd be open-and-shut. A clear retaliation for Beelzebub's own betrayal that the Court wouldn't see any need to investigate."

"So it seems," said Uriel. "Very well, the Choir will agree to provide you the means to eliminate Beelzebub. From there, it's up to you to ingratiate yourself with the Court."

"Good, then it's settled."

"Now that we've gotten that out of the way, where can we find Lucifer?" asked Uriel. "The Choir is anxious to get their hands on him."

"He's in Limbo."

Uriel's mouth opened in a moment of realization. "Ahh yes, of course. The place for all refuse. Just toss him in the void and pretend he no longer exists. Good, I'll inform the Choir immediately of this."

"Don't move just yet. We have to time this simultaneously," said Asmodeus. "Beelzebub gets hit in a public display and that means no eyes will be on any dimensional breaches. Gives Kushiel the chance he needs to go in and capture Lucifer once and for all."

Uriel nodded. "As you wish. Who is it you plan to frame for this attack?"

Asmodeus grinned. "Who do you think? None other than Lucifer's loyal attack dog. Belial would be the obvious suspect in such a move and he's currently on Earth."

"Which makes him vulnerable."

"Precisely. You grab him, put an appropriate whammy on him, and then send him on a kamikaze mission to kill Beelzebub in a very public manner," said Asmodeus. "While that's going on, Kushiel goes into Limbo and grabs Lucifer."

A wide grin spread on Uriel's face. "You know, Asmodeus, I think we just might become friends after all."

Asmodeus smiled back, but raised a cautioning finger. "Easy there, old boy. You wouldn't want it getting out that you're buddying around with the next Satan."

CHAPTER 23

Anael had used the coin Death gave her and now she was back in Charon's ferry. She still didn't know exactly where they were headed. Death had only told her that she'd know what to do once she met the person she was looking for. Her assumption was that it was Metatron, but something about the coin he gave her made her think that wasn't it.

The fog parted and they came to a small island with a shack sitting there. Anael nodded her thanks to Charon and flew over to the shack's lone door. She knocked a few times, but no one answered. Taking a chance, she reached for the knob and turned it.

It was unlocked and she was able to step inside. Despite how small it was on the outside, it seemed impossibly larger on the inside. The shack on the outside only looked to be one story. But inside, the ceiling went far higher, stretching up past Anael's ability to see the top. The walls were all lined with different varieties of clocks. Some of them were ancient, some were more modern with digital numbers and displays, and there were even several hourglasses scattered on some random shelves.

Anael walked through the maze of timepieces and came

to a staircase. She descended the steps and then up against the far wall, she saw a bench with a child sitting at it. The child spun on the stool—it was a girl no more than ten years old and she wore glasses with a selection of moveable magnifying lenses.

"Who're you?" asked the girl.

"My name's Anael. I was sent here by Death."

The girl frowned. "That's a load of crap." She turned on her stool and went back to her work.

Anael moved closer to the bench and saw the girl was working on a watch. The angel was now beginning to figure out just exactly who it was Death had sent her to meet. Anael looked down at the girl, staring at her.

"You're Khronus, aren't you?" she asked. "Master of time."

The girl huffed. "Yeah, and you're an angel who's in way, *way* over her head if you're coming to speak to me."

"Please, if you could just listen to me," said Anael. "If Death sent me to you, then it must have been for a reason. He said you're the only one who can help the Morningstar."

Khronus looked up from the watch she was fixing. "The Morningstar? You're here because of Lucifer?"

Anael nodded. "He's gotten himself in an interesting predicament. At first, I thought finding the Scribe would help him, so I thought perhaps that's where Death was sending me. Instead, Charon took me here."

"So Death thought I could or *would* help Lucifer out of whatever fix he's gotten himself?" asked Khronus. "And just why would I do that?"

Anael shrugged. "I really don't know. He mentioned the Apocalypse, but said things weren't right. Other than that, he was pretty vague."

Khronus gave an annoyed scoff. "Sounds just like him." She paused in her work and set down her tweezers. "What about the Apocalypse?"

"He said that Lucifer would be bound, but only after the Horsemen were summoned. And that hasn't happened," said Anael.

Khronus spun her stool around and hopped off it. She began walking away from the bench and as she moved, it was like she was climbing an invisible staircase, moving all the way towards the top of her home.

Anael had to follow with her wings, and once she caught up with Khronus, the time-master was staring at a few clocks. These were of a particularly unique design. There wasn't just one set of hands, but several. And there weren't any numbers on them, only symbols that Anael had never seen before. Just trying to make sense of them began to give the angel a headache.

"He's right, the timetable's off…" muttered Khronus.

"For the Apocalypse prophecy? When is it supposed to happen?" asked Anael.

Khronus shook her head. "No, it doesn't work that way. People often think of prophecies as if they're a map that must be followed, but if that were true, then what would be the point in living if everything you will ever do has been pre-ordained?"

"Then how *does* it work?" asked Anael.

"It's more like a series of causalities and probabilities," said Khronus. "If you put your hand in fire, your hand will burn. But you don't think of that as destiny. It's the same thing with these prophecies. If certain events happen, then other events will also happen as a reaction to them. Or at least they have a high probability of happening."

"But they could also *not* happen?" asked Anael.

Khronus nodded. "And that's essentially the basis of the Manifold."

"What's the Manifold?" asked Anael.

"People have come up with many names for it. The many-worlds interpretation, the multiverse, parallel dimensions, alternate realities, elseworlds, and on and on. I've always just called it the Manifold."

Khronus turned around and clapped her hands together horizontally. As she separated them, the image of a tree formed between her palms.

"Think of your universe as a tree. All these little branches are just the various dimensional planes connected to your universe. Heaven, Hell, Purgatory, Earth, Asgard, Olympus…you get the idea." Khronus then clapped her hands over the tree, this time vertically. When her hands came apart again, now there were a series of trees. "But a forest contains more than one tree. And though some trees may look very similar, there are little differences in them, if you look closely enough. So a prophecy just states a situation and then one possible outcome. But in the Manifold, each of these 'world trees' is one where every possible outcome has occurred."

"What's that mean for this world?"

"For every cause, there's an effect. For every action, a reaction," said Khronus. "If tree overgrowth occurs, it becomes too heavy for the branches to bear the weight, and the branches start to fall. What you call the Apocalypse is more like the beginning of a new epoch. Existence doesn't end in these prophecies, does it?"

Anael shook her head.

"The path that your world is on is similar to overgrowth. And if things aren't changed, then it could lead to collapse," said Khronus. "In other words, the decimation of your entire universe."

Anael hesitated for a moment to process what Khronus has just told her. Then she shook her head, unable to truly grasp the vastness of such a concept. "That's not possible. Planets can die, species can become extinct, but an entire *universe*?"

Khronus gave Anael a stern look. "Do you really think it *hasn't* happened before?"

The angel was at a loss for words. Was it really possible that everything happening was jeopardizing her entire world? The literal end of all things? It was a far greater catastrophe than any apocalyptic prophecy she'd ever read.

"Something should be done. Something *has* to be done," said Anael. "I doubt Death would send me to you not knowing all of this."

"Oh, I'm sure he knows *all* of this, and I'm positive he *thinks* he knows what can be done to fix it," said Khronus. "Death's always been arrogant enough to think that he knows more than everyone else. But I'm not so sure what's happening to your universe is something that should be stopped."

"But why?" asked Anael. "If the universe ends, then don't *you* end with it?"

Khronus gave a giggle. "Do you really think I'm part of your universe? Oh, honey. You angels call yourselves celestials, which I honestly think is pretty cute. I exist beyond the scope of any single universe. I'm a constant across the Manifold."

"Do you even care what happens to my world?"

Khronus waved her hands and the images of the forest

vanished. "Not particularly, no. Another universe will eventually come around. They usually do."

"In other words, I've wasted my time coming to you for help?"

"I never said that, I just said it doesn't matter to me one way or the other," said Khronus. "But since Death sent you here, seems he's got an interest in seeing your world survive. So I can give you the means to help your Lucifer."

Khronus moved back down the structure, again as if descending invisible steps. Anael flew after, not sure what was going to come next. When she met up with Khronus, the girl was examining a watch with a sundial on it.

"Time isn't rigid, like many think," said Khronus. "It's fluid, like a river. You can change its direction, constrict its flow, block it completely, whatever. You just need the tools to do so. But the spells to manipulate time are dangerous and shouldn't be trifled with. It's why we've kept them locked away."

Khronus handed Anael the sundial. The angel accepted the gift and examined it, turning it over and over in her hands, running her fingers over the stony surface of the dial.

"This isn't all of it, just one piece of the puzzle," said Khronus. "The sundial just acts as an anchor. But to traverse the Manifold, you'll need a unique spellbook. For the sake of security, the pages have been scattered across worlds."

"How do I find them?" asked Anael.

Khronus beckoned with her hand. "Bend down closer to me."

Anael knelt down so she and the girl were eye-level. And then Khronus delivered a powerful slap that toppled the angel. Just as Anael was about to protest, her mind suddenly flashed with new knowledge, the location of the pages that they needed.

"That's how," said Khronus. "But I have to warn you—these are powerful forces I'm giving you access to. If you're not careful, you may end up doing even greater damage than the destruction of your universe."

"And what exactly do we do with this power?" asked Anael.

Khronus shrugged. "You'll have to figure that one out yourself. But you can't do it alone. You're going to need the Morningstar beside you if you want to change his fate and the fate of your world."

Anael nodded. "I know you don't care what happens to us, but thank you for giving us a chance."

"Don't thank me, just fix your timeline," said Khronus. "I will."

With that, Anael left Khronus's home. She stepped through the door and stood outside the shack once again. Charon and his ferry were waiting for her, exactly where they'd been when she entered. She flew over to the boat and touched down inside.

"Did you get what you need?" asked Charon.

Anael examined the sundial. "I hope so. Now I just need to get to Lucifer before it's too late."

CHAPTER 24

How long had Lucifer been in Limbo? Could have been mere minutes by the standards of Earth that he'd recently grown accustomed to. Or it could have been a few thousand years. There was no concrete way for him to judge for himself.

Chances were high that Belial had already begun work on a liberation plan. Part of Lucifer hoped he wouldn't bother. Once he got out of Limbo, that would no doubt make him a target for Heaven. At least here, he was safe—bored, but safe.

But another part of him couldn't wait for that tear to appear in the fabric of this reality. A chance to escape and exact vengeance on everyone who had put him in this position—Asmodeus, Samedi, Beelzebub, Uriel…

"Aren't you forgetting someone?"

Lucifer was surprised to hear another voice echoing in the blackness of Limbo. The voice came from all directions and no matter how many times Lucifer tried to turn, he couldn't find the source.

"Who else is in here?" asked Lucifer. "If this is a joke, I'm not amused."

"The only joke here is what you've become."

LUCIFER JUDGED

Flames suddenly appeared before Lucifer and he stepped back, his eyes briefly blinded by the sudden introduction of light to this realm. The fire took the shape of a winged figure. A very familiar one—he had Lucifer's features, the same dark hair, the same feathered wings. But where he differed was the clothing. This new Lucifer was dressed in the white robes he'd worn when he was still in Heaven. And also the eyes—his other self had the cobalt-blue eyes of an angel.

"The only one responsible for all of this is you," said the younger Lucifer.

"I see I've started to go crazy," said Lucifer.

"If only. That'd make things more convenient. But unfortunately, every decision you've made has been with all your faculties intact. Which makes it all the more pathetic."

"And what do you know?" asked Lucifer, turning away from his doppelgänger.

"I know you were going to expose the lie. Reveal the truth so that angels wouldn't have to live under the boot of the Choir. What happened to all that?"

"It wouldn't have worked. They would have all rejected the notion. Anael wouldn't even hear me out when I tried to tell her. That's something you'll learn."

The angel scoffed. "One person takes some effort to convince and so you decide, 'nah, this is too much work.' Nice to know you were able to stick to your convictions."

"Explaining the concept of a godless universe to an angel is like explaining quantum physics to a kitten. Even if you're able to get through it all, they still won't understand."

"Angels are incapable of grasping such difficult concepts, is that what you're saying?" asked the young angel.

"No, I'm saying they're incapable of grasping *this* concept."

The younger Lucifer folded his arms and just stared intently at his older counterpart. "*We* seemed to understand it just fine. So did Metatron, so did Abraxas, even Pyriel."

"And with the exception of us, they were all driven stark-raving bonkers," said Lucifer.

"Weren't you the one who once said that if free will wasn't possible for angels then you never would have been able to rebel?" asked the younger version. "What happened to that?"

"Maybe I wasn't thinking straight. When I said that, I'd spent a significant amount of time locked inside my tower with nothing but my thoughts to keep me company," said Lucifer.

"Or maybe you're just a quitter. Afraid to actually commit to the work necessary for a true revolution."

"I never *wanted* a revolution!" shouted Lucifer. "All I ever wanted was to bring the truth to the rest of Heaven. I was forced into this position."

The young Lucifer stared at his older self for a few moments in silence. Then he pantomimed wiping away tears.

"Oh boo-fucking-hoo, woe is me, things didn't turn out the way I'd hoped!" The younger version shook his head. "Will you grow a spine already and stop feeling sorry for yourself? So you didn't get what you wanted, oh well. Own it and move on."

"What do you think the trial was about?"

"You evading responsibility, like always. You're still leaving your fate up to others to decide. Heaven, Hell, Purgatory, whatever. Find your own path out of this mess for once. Maybe then, you'll finally find peac—"

LUCIFER JUDGED

The younger Lucifer was suddenly cut off as something tore through him, his image vanishing. In the spot where he once stood was now a break in reality and a bright, white light seeped through the tear.

A massive figure stepped through, his body wrapped in leather and his azure eyes burning brightly within the dark confines of his mask, chains hanging from his wrists.

"Hello, Morningstar," said Kushiel. "The time has come for you to welcome my embrace."

"Are you out of your mind?" asked Lucifer. "If you go through with this, it'll only reignite the war!"

"Oh no, we're operating under new rules now." Kushiel thrust one massive arm forward and the chains flew off his limb. They took on a life of their own, slithering towards Lucifer's body.

The Morningstar jumped over one of the chains and grabbed another as it came within reach, holding it back as if it were a snake trying to bite his face off. New rules? This had the stink of Asmodeus's treachery. Only he would be bold enough to make a deal with Heaven after everything.

A chain snagged Lucifer's leg and pulled him up, holding him in an inverted position. Twin hellfire blades formed in Lucifer's hands and he used them to break the chain and free himself. As he cut through the ethereal metal, he heard a high-pitched whine come from the chain, almost like a cry of agony.

Lucifer's wings emerged and he righted himself in the void. The two swords vanished and he made a wide swoop with his arm. A barrage of hellfire projectiles were fired, buffeting the massive angel.

Kushiel raised his arms for protection, his chains responding in kind and trying to deflect as many of the projectiles as they could. Many were still able to get through despite the valiant effort.

With Kushiel distracted, Lucifer circled behind him. Hellfire coalesced in the Morningstar's clasped hands. A massive spear formed in his grip and raised it above his head and thrust it down into Kushiel's back.

Kushiel's chest jerked forward from the impact and he let out a loud groan of pain. The angel slumped over the spear and stayed there for a few moments. Lucifer didn't trust that this meant the end of Heaven's jailer and he was already starting to form a hellfire sword to be ready for the next attack.

The angel's hand moved. He lumbered to a standing position and turned to Lucifer. Kushiel's fingers wrapped around the spear and he slowly pulled it all the way through until it came out of his body. The angel examined the spear, his eyes burning with cobalt fire. The spear itself glowed and slowly, the hellfire began to be overtaken by Kushiel's own soulfire, the color going from yellow to blue.

The spear then broke down and the energy flowed into Kushiel's hands. As it did, the chains came alive, animated by soulfire. They went after Lucifer again, and try as he might, the Morningstar couldn't fend them off. Quickly, he was tangled up in the chains, being bound to Kushiel's will.

Their weight seemed to grow with each passing moment. Lucifer's wings couldn't fight their pull and they dragged him down. He was forced to his feet and still attempted to remain defiant. An aura of hellfire surrounded his body and he tried to use that to put off the effects of the chains. It gave him some slight resistance, but just at first.

Kushiel tugged on his end of the chains and Lucifer lost his footing, collapsing to his knees. He still tried to stand, but the chains wrapped around him, forming shackles around his wrists, ankles, and neck. Kushiel yanked on the chains, pulling Lucifer right over to him.

The warden grabbed the chains attached to the neck restraint. He held Lucifer by them, hefting him into the air and grinned as his eyes burned with bright, blue energy.

"Stop struggling, Lucifer—you're mine now," said Kushiel.

Lucifer spat. The small glob of saliva struck Kushiel between his eyes and slowly slid down his leather mask. He gave a short chuckle in response, clearly amused by Lucifer's continued resistance.

"Ever the heretic, defiant even in the face of utter defeat," said Kushiel. "You know, you are the only prisoner to have escaped my embrace. How I've missed you, Lucifer. And the fun we shall have now that we're together again."

"Mark my words, Kushiel, there *will* be retaliation for this," said Lucifer. "The Court—"

"Your fellow traitors in the Infernal Court are no concern. They have other matters to worry about right now," said Kushiel.

"What do you mean by that? What's the Choir done this time?" asked Lucifer.

Kushiel's chuckle sounded like the rumble of an earthquake. "Such a shame you'll never know. You're going to be locked away for all eternity, Morningstar. We're going to be together forever, you and I."

The angel's wings emerged from his back, big and bulky just as he was, and wrapped with leather. The wings wrapped around both him and his prisoner. Lucifer felt the hope fading from him as they vanished in a bright flash of light.

When the light had faded, Lucifer was alone once again. But no longer in Limbo. Now he was in a familiar cell, with a clear ceiling so he could see the perfect blue sky and picturesque white clouds of Elysium high above.

He was back in Gehenna. Right back where the revolution had begun all those eons ago. All his attempts to escape this place and the weight of Heaven's oppression, everything he'd done in the time since, now it all seemed like little more than a wasted effort.

Lucifer slumped down to his knees, despair overtaking him on a level it never had before. Hell had turned its back on him, Heaven had taken him prisoner again, what more was there for him to do?

CHAPTER 25

Belial's eyes slowly opened. His lids were heavy and his body felt sluggish. Why, he didn't know. It was as if he was coming out of a daze. And for some reason, he woke lying on a stone surface. The last thing he remembered was speaking with Lucifer, and then he returned to Earth. He had been doing research on spells to breach Limbo to save his master, and once he'd discovered one that was both capable and sufficiently covert, he would have recruited help.

And after that...

His mind was blank. He couldn't remember what came next. And for the first time, he noticed he wasn't in Lucifer's home library. Belial pulled himself off the ground and he stumbled as he tried to stand. He planted his hand to prevent himself from completely collapsing.

His head was swimming. Why couldn't he remember what had happened? And where *was* he?

Belial realized there was a dampness below his hand. He looked and saw that his hand was resting in a thick, black liquid. The demon examined his hand and the viscous substance that now coated it. He took a sniff and realized what it was.

191

Blood.

Specifically, *demonic* blood.

Belial tried standing again, moving slower this time in hopes it would stop him from collapsing once more. It had worked and he was able to stand. The pooled blood stretched out into a trail leading across the stone floor.

He was in a room. Stone walls and a ceiling with wall-mounted torches providing flickering light. Belial followed the trail to heavy, wooden doors. He pushed them open and went inside.

This was a bedroom with a massive, king-size bed. A fireplace attached to one wall had smoldering, blackened logs. The blood led right up to the bed and when Belial sniffed the air, he picked up the stench of death.

The sheets were in disarray. Belial examined the bedding and found the sheets were stained with the black blood. But there was no body. What there was, however, was an appendage. Long, thin, and chitinous. Belial had a pretty good idea who all this blood had belonged to.

On the other side of the bed, Belial found the end of the trail. A dismembered body—not humanoid, but in-sectoid. Gossamer wings were torn to shreds and scattered about like confetti. And then, a body like a giant fly, minus its head.

The head had rolled under the bed. Belial knelt down and reached for it. He pulled it from its hiding place and confirmed that he was indeed looking into the now-lifeless eyes of Beelzebub.

"Seems you got what you deserved, traitor," muttered Belial. But what did any of this have to do with him? And how did he even get here?

Noises came from outside the room. Belial went to the

door and pushed it open. What he found on the other side was Beelzebub's guard, clad in their chitinous armor and holding hellfire spears that were aimed at him, their points blazing.

Waking in Beelzebub's castle with the Hell Lord's dismembered body lying nearby, no memory of how he got there, and guards waiting right outside the doors? This certainly didn't seem like a coincidence.

To add insult to injury, Belial realized he was still holding Beelzebub's head.

"Right…" he began, "would you believe this isn't what it looks like?"

"He still has the Lord's head!" shouted one of the guards.

"Surrender now, Belial, by the authority of Lord Beelzebub!"

Belial looked down at the head. "I doubt his authority has much reach anymore."

"Attack!"

Belial threw Beelzebub's head at the guard who shouted the command, striking him in the head and knocking him down. The demon held out his hands and hellfire crackled in his palms. He forged twin cutlasses and readied himself for battle.

With the exception of the one he'd already knocked down, the rest of the guards hesitated. Belial's reputation in Hell was legendary. He was one of the fiercest warriors during the war and could have been granted a place on the Infernal Court himself, but he didn't want it. Instead, he remained loyal to Lucifer and Lucifer alone. None of these soldiers wanted to test their own skills against his.

The choice wasn't theirs, though. Their master had

been assassinated and Belial seemed the likely culprit. Their duty was to bring him in or kill him during the attempt. But even demons were capable of fear.

Belial wasn't about to wait for them to find their courage. He rushed into the fray, his cutlasses moving like flaming blurs as he cut through their weapons, armor, and flesh. Blood splattered against the walls and the floors, body parts flying across the castle halls.

The guards were little match for the demon warrior. Though he didn't choose this fight, Belial was relishing the opportunity to cut loose. In his time on Earth, Lucifer had urged restraint, even when Belial worked with Odysseus Black. This was a matter of life or death, and Belial allowed the beast inside to go off its leash.

Their screams echoed off the castle walls. For Belial, the sound was intoxicating. The heat of battle provided a better rush than any drug ever could. But like any endeavor, it quickly started to grow weary. Calling these demons soldiers seemed a disservice to the term. They were cowardly, incompetent punks who were probably forced into the position out of demons randomly selected from the population. Their training—if they had even undertaken any—was laughable. Their martial skill was nonexistent.

It wasn't long before Belial was covered from head to toe in blood, the gore sliding down his form, their essence dripping off the edges of his blades. He stuck his tongue out and licked some of the blood off his own lips. The rush had ended too soon and he wasn't sure he was ready for it to be over. He wanted a *real* challenge, something these sycophants were incapable of.

What few guards remained were moving away from the demon, backing out into the main hall and down the twin staircases that led down to the ground floor. Belial went to the edge of the balcony and stared down at them.

"You're pathetic," he said. "I've seen more effort from the talking monkeys of Earth than you so-called demons have displayed."

The doors to the castle's main hall opened and in strode a new figure. Belial cocked his head to the side and watched at a demon in a red suit entered, his long, black hair spilling down over his shoulders, crimson wings tucked in.

"I wouldn't be too hard on the boys, Belial," said Asmodeus. "There are few in any realm who can match both your expertise or your bloodlust."

"What are you doing here?" asked Belial.

"I live here," said Asmodeus. "Beelzebub was kind enough to offer me a home here. You know, since Cocytus is gone and my realm is under new management."

"So Beelzebub rewards traitors now?"

"Traitor? *Moi?*" Asmodeus feigned offense. "Such harsh words, old friend. I'm truly hurt. Especially when it seems that the real traitor in this castle is *you.*"

"I had nothing to do with Beelzebub's death," said Belial.

"Then what were you doing with his head?"

"I found him like that."

"Well, *that* sounds convincing," said Asmodeus. "And why did you slaughter the guards when they found you?"

"It was self-defense."

"You struck the first blow."

"Fine, it was *anticipatory* self-defense," said Belial. "I knew where the situation was headed and acted appropriately."

"Do you have any explanation for what you were

even *doing* in Lord Beelzebub's castle?" asked Asmodeus. "I don't recall the two of you having a particularly close relationship. Matter of fact, you haven't really had much of a relationship with *anyone* in Hell, save the Morningstar."

"I have no idea how I ended up here. The last thing I remember is being on Earth, in Lucifer's home. And then somehow, I woke up here. I found the blood. Followed the trail, and discovered Beelzebub."

"No memory of how you ended up unannounced in the home of a Hell Lord you had motive to murder?" asked Asmodeus. "As alibis go, I daresay that one seems to have some holes in it."

"Think what you want. I have more important things to do."

Asmodeus folded his arms over his chest, narrowing his eyes. "And what makes you think you're going anywhere? You've murdered a Hell Lord and you need to be held accountable for your actions."

"If you wish to stop me, then you're more than welcome to try." Belial slammed the cutlasses together and they merged into a single sword with a flaming blade.

Asmodeus lowered his arms and slid his hands into his pockets with a sigh. "Do we *really* have to go through all that, Belial? Can't you just be a good boy and surrender peacefully?"

"Hell no."

Belial jumped from the balcony overlooking the main hall and dove towards Asmodeus. He held the flaming sword in an inverted grip, prepared to drive it through the demon's head. Asmodeus remained calm. With a graceful swoop, he raised one arm and held out his hand, with his fingers outstretched.

The warrior found himself stopped in mid-fall. Asmodeus held Belial firmly in place. Belial struggled against the hold Asmodeus had on his body, but wasn't able to break it.

"Believing that brute force is the best solution to every problem has always been your kryptonite," said Asmodeus. "All that time spent with Lucifer, and one would think you would have learned at least *something*. But I suppose a beat-down old guard dog like you isn't capable of learning new tricks."

Belial growled in response to Asmodeus's taunts and kept trying to break the hold. His muscles barely even twitched in response to the effort. Asmodeus had always been a very skilled mage, but this seemed like something more. In the past, not even he would have been able to hold Belial with such little effort.

Asmodeus raised his hand and Belial was thrown up to the ceiling, smashing into it. Laughter echoed through the hall and Asmodeus then moved his hand from side to side, and Belial was thrown into each wall, mimicking the movements of Asmodeus's hand. For the finale, Asmodeus clapped his hands together and Belial was driven into the ground, surrounded by a crater the shape of his body.

Belial still couldn't move and now every inch of his form screamed in pain. Asmodeus knelt down beside the demon and tapped him on his bald head. Asmodeus leaned in close and whispered.

"I want you to know this is nothing personal. I'm just doing what needed to be done."

"Feels like you're talking about something more than Beelzebub," muttered Belial.

Asmodeus gave a shrug. "I'm not sure what you're going

on about." He stood and turned to the remaining guards. "Take this traitor to the dungeons. Lord Beelzebub's assassination must be avenged."

CHAPTER 26

From Khronus's home, Charon then took Anael to Earth. She wasn't ready to return to Heaven yet, in case her departure had gone noticed. But she also couldn't just walk right into Hell without permission. She was unaware of what had transpired in the trial since she left, so she had to hope that it was still going on and she could reach Lucifer before a verdict or sentencing.

Charon's boat came to a stop just off the coast of Lake Michigan. From there, Anael's wings carried her into the air and she flew the short distance from the boat to Rush Street and the location of Lust. She expected Belial to still be in Hell, but Mara had responsibilities on Earth. And strangely enough, that demon was the only one Anael could trust at the moment.

Anael dropped between buildings and retracted her wings. It was night and judging by the length of the line outside the club, had to be a weekend. She wasn't even sure how long in Earth time she'd been gone.

She walked past the crowd of people waiting to be let in and went to the front entrance. There were two demons working as bouncers, identified by their pale, yellow eyes.

And as soon as they saw her unnatural blue ones, they knew exactly what she was, too.

"Your kind's not welcome here," said one of the bouncers.

"I'm not here to cause trouble, I'm here to speak with your mistress. Can you just tell her that Anael needs to speak with her?"

The bouncer looked at his partner and gave a nod. The other bouncer took out a cell phone and stepped away to speak. He came back a moment later and shook his head.

"That's a no," said the one Anael had been speaking with.

"Call her back, tell her it's important."

The bouncer glanced over each shoulder. "Do I look like I've got feathers sticking out my ass?"

Anael sighed and shook her head.

"See any floating rings above my head?"

"No," she said in a flat tone.

"Then what makes you think you can order me around?"

"Please, just listen to me," said Anael. "This is very important. It concerns the Morningstar."

He scoffed at that and looked at his partner, who also wore a knowing smile. They both began chuckling at her words. When he looked at Anael and saw the confusion on his face, his laughter subsided, but the grin remained. One that reeked of smug satisfaction.

"You haven't heard, have you?" he asked. "Lucifer's gone."

"Gone?" she repeated.

He nodded. "They found him guilty and sentenced him to Limbo."

Anael was at a loss. His gambit had failed. She was always suspicious of just how fair such a trial could be, so she wasn't surprised by the outcome. More the complication it created. Limbo was a place of very little security and leaving him trapped in that place meant it'd be easy for someone to break him out.

Or capture him and take him elsewhere.

"Then it's all the more important I speak with Mara," said Anael.

The bouncer sighed and stepped closer towards her. His size dwarfed hers by a good amount. He folded massive arms over his stone-like chest. "You got a hearing problem or something, lady?" He jerked an arm up, pointing his thumb at the club. "You're *not* getting in here. Now run away before you piss me off."

Anael sighed and cracked her knuckles. "I hoped we could do this without violence, but I suppose not…"

He chuckled and placed his hands on his hips. The smile transformed into a sneer. "Do your worst, bitch."

The doors of Lust were blown off their hinges and flew inward. The guests closest to the doors were struck by flying splinters and chunks of wood. People fled from the entrance with cries of surprise.

The bouncer lay on his back. He had been the projectile that destroyed the doors and he laid motionless on his back. His eyes were open, fixed in a state of shock.

Anael moved through the broken entrance after him, stepping calmly and deliberately, moving around the splintered pieces of wood. She stared down at him and sneered the same way he'd done just moments earlier.

"You just *had* to be difficult, didn't you?"

The second bouncer thought this would be a good opportunity to strike. He moved cautiously after her, taking an empty barstool and raising it above his head. Once he was within reach, he brought the stool down on her from behind.

Anael slid and jumped to the side. The demon's follow-through sent him stumbling once he missed the target. He quickly regained his footing and swung at her again. She grabbed the stool with one hand and tore it from his grasp. Anael swung it back and struck the side of his head with the stool.

The demon wobbled, but didn't fall. He was a stubborn one and stood his ground. Anael felt it would make things simpler if she didn't use any overt angelic powers like her wings or soulfire, so she readied herself as he prepared to strike again.

He moved in with a few punches that were clearly telegraphed and easy for Anael to evade. She was toying with him a bit, letting him believe he had the upper hand in this fight. He tried a few more swings, but she dodged these, too.

"This really isn't necessary," she said. "Just tell Mara I need to speak to her and we can stop this right now."

"Like I'm dumb enough to fall for an angel's trick!"

He came at her again, but by this point, Anael was finished playing. She grabbed his fist as he tried to punch her and pulled his arm straight, then slammed her elbow on it. A crack echoed even louder than the club music. Anael grabbed his head and drove it through the wall. He went limp at that moment, hanging unconscious from the hole his neck was still stuck in.

Anael left him there and began her walk to the stairs. The crowd parted for her, no one wanting to take a chance of landing on her bad side. She climbed all the stairs until she reached Mara's office on the top floor, overlooking the club. There was a demon standing guard in front of the door and Anael stretched out her fingers in case she had to get violent again.

This demon was smarter than the others—or maybe he'd been told to stand down. Whatever the case, he simply opened the door and gestured for her to go inside. Anael didn't waste any words on him and just walked through the door.

The door closed behind her and Anael saw Mara standing at the windows, looking out over her club. "You owe me for those damages."

"Maybe if your men had just let me through, that could have been avoided," said Anael.

"Whatever." Mara turned from the windows. It was clear from her gaze that she wasn't interested in playing nice. "Lucifer's gone and you're no longer working for Eden. There's no reason I should have to tolerate your shit."

"That's why I came. I think I have a way to help Lucifer."

Mara scoffed. "Oh please. You bailed on him in the middle of the trial and now you claim you want to help him? Way I see it, this is all your fault."

"I had no choice," said Anael. "The Divine Choir pulled me away. If I'd defied them, there's no telling how far they would have taken things."

"And they've sanctioned your appearance here?"

"Well...no..."

"I see. So exactly *how* do you know which orders you can and can't defy?" asked Mara. "Is it like weekends are Defiance Days? Or is there some sort of chart detailing when you can and can't go against their will?"

Anael sighed. "I know you're angry and you have a right to be—"

"Damn fucking straight I do."

"Just hear me out and when this is all over, you can insult me all you like," said Anael. "I know Lucifer is in Limbo, but I believe I have the means to make all this right. A way to fix things so that none of this has to happen."

Mara narrowed her eyes, but they still held a bit of inquisitiveness. "What are you talking about?"

"I've gone above the Choir's heads, so to speak. I spoke with Khronus."

"Bullshit," said Mara. "Nobody talks to Khronus."

"If what she's told me is true, we can fix everything. But to do that, I need to get Lucifer out of Limbo."

"Right, I'm sure the Court will love that," said Mara.

"By the time the Court or the Choir figures out what I'm doing, it will be too late to stop me," said Anael.

Mara shrugged. "So do it. You know where he is, so why are you still here? You need my permission or something?"

"More like your help," said Anael. "The Choir has restricted my travel abilities. I can't move between realms under my own power. I came here through the Styx and I don't have any way to summon Charon again."

"So you need me to open a portal for you." Mara chuckled. "Oh, this is rich."

"If I have to find someone else to help me, then I will. But I'm here now and you claim to be a servant of Lucifer's, so why don't you live up to that characterization?"

Mara paused and considered the situation. "I would do anything for the Morningstar. But what assurances do I have that you've got his best interests at heart? Certainly wouldn't be the first time you've screwed him over."

"I took his case, didn't I?" asked Anael. "I've seen first-hand how the Choir's claims of serving the Presence don't seem to add up to the reality of the situation."

"So now you believe Lucifer?"

Anael sighed. "I don't know whether or not the Presence exists. But I'm certain that even if he does, the Choir isn't operating under his direction."

Mara folded her arms as she studied Anael's face, trying to process what she just said. "You're serious, aren't you? No bullshit?"

Anael nodded. "I don't think anyone really knows the full story. And I believe Lucifer shouldn't be scapegoated anymore just so Heaven can have an existential enemy. Help me."

Mara didn't give a response right away. She was still working through her thought processes. Anael didn't try to push her, but her patience was also beginning to wane. If they didn't act soon, there was no telling what would happen. The Choir wanted Lucifer and they might have already gotten him.

"Okay, I'll do it," she said. "But if anyone comes after me for this, I'm telling them that you tortured me."

"Do whatever you have to, Mara. Just get it done," said Anael.

"You want to rush me, you can find someone else."

"Fine, you're right, I'm sorry," said Anael. "I'm just… frustrated with this whole thing."

"Welcome to my world," said Mara. "Let's prepare a spell to breach Limbo."

CHAPTER 27

I n the basement of Lust, surrounded by instruments of torture, sadism, and magical artifacts, Mara completed her preparations. The spell to open a portal to Limbo was a simple one. Had Anael's own powers not been restricted by the Choir, she could have easily opened one herself.

The sigil Mara had spray-painted on the stone floor was a circle. Inside the circle, she drew the symbol for Limbo in the Dimoori Sheol, the language of the damned. Even just looking at the language caused Anael to instinctively flinch. The Choir's indoctrination against demons ran deep and though she knew intellectually that her and Mara were on the same side, old habits died hard.

Mara directed Anael to stand in the center of the circle, and she did so—albeit apprehensively. Instinctual revulsion kept screaming in the back of her mind that this was all a trap. Once Anael was in position, Mara began chanting in the demonic language.

Anael felt her insides being pulled towards the sigil. She looked down and saw the lines of the symbol beginning to move, rotating and swirling ever faster until they became a vortex into a black void. Anael was pulled into the center, her soulform becoming one with the spinning lines until everything was a complete blur.

The feeling of being pulled into a vortex continued on for some time, though Anael wasn't sure how long. It then suddenly stopped and she stood in complete darkness. The spell had worked—she was in Limbo.

The sudden restoration of her equilibrium was a shock to her body and she almost felt like retching. Anael breathed slowly, swallowing air—or whatever passed for air in this place—until her body had settled down.

The darkness of Limbo extended in all directions and seemingly with no end. Anael held up a hand and an orb of soulfire formed just above her open palm. It split into several smaller orbs and they flew in different directions.

The orbs didn't provide any real illumination, as if they weren't capable of even casting any light. That wasn't their only purpose, though—they were also scouts of sorts. Anael was using them to try to find Lucifer in this endless void.

Not long after they left Anael's presence, they returned, reforging into one orb and moving in front of her face. Anael gently touched the orb and it was reabsorbed into her body.

Nothing.

Was she too late? Had Belial already gotten Lucifer out? Or even worse…?

"I thought you'd find your way here eventually."

Anael spun on her heel to face the familiar voice. She didn't need to see him to know who she was facing off against. Uriel stepped forth through the darkness, his hands clasped calmly behind his back and his wings folded behind his shoulders.

"What are you doing here?" she asked.

"I should ask you the same thing," said Uriel. "Correct me if I'm wrong, but didn't the Choir forbid you from leaving Elysium?"

"Where's Lucifer?" asked Anael.

"He's where he belongs, and where you'll be going soon." Uriel clicked his tongue. "I'm very disappointed in you, Anael. You had an opportunity to really make a name for yourself. To climb the celestial ladder, as it were."

"If only I followed you blindly?" she asked.

He shrugged. "And what's so wrong with that? I'm on the fast-track, my dear. I've given the Choir some of the best gifts they could ever ask for." Uriel raised a finger to count each of them. "The Morningstar is no longer an issue, there's soon to be a new Satan, and I'm about to bring them another traitor."

"What new Satan?" asked Anael.

Her response came in the form of a stinging, burning pain across her back. Anael struck the ground and looked over her shoulder. Asmodeus stood there, a hellfire sword in his grip.

"Such a pleasure to see you again," he said.

"Asmodeus…" she muttered. "You idiot, you think the Infernal Court will just turn things over to you?"

"Cross's days are numbered, now that one of Lucifer's followers retaliated against the Court. Poor Beelzebub has been assassinated by Belial," said Asmodeus with a grin. "But fortunately, there's a prime contender to take over the now-lordless realm."

The plot was clear now. Asmodeus and Uriel were working together for their own ends—Uriel becomes the Choir's new golden boy, Asmodeus gets one step closer to becoming the King of Hell, and the Choir was now able to paint Asmodeus as the new existential threat to Heaven's existence.

"This won't stand," she said.

"And who's going to stop it?" asked Uriel. "What are you going to do, tattle to the Divine Choir? They support my plan. Even praised my initiative."

It truly was broken. Every aspect of celestial order that Anael had spent her entire life believing in. Never in service of some sort of divine plan or benign deity, but all of it for the sake of a group of beings who wanted nothing less than absolute control over everything.

Anael was tired of it. She channeled the anger into her hands, forging a soulfire sword of her own, the blade itself a raging, azure inferno. She went for Asmodeus first, who was barely able to react to her speed in time to block. Their flaming swords locked and Anael stared daggers, her eyes burning with the same intensity as her weapon. Asmodeus's grin remained ever-present. He seemed to enjoy her anger.

Asmodeus pulled his sword back and thrust forward. Anael parried and countered, landing a blow on his arm. He drew back to assess the damage. And Anael went in for another strike, her wings lifting her above his head. She brought the sword around in an arc and dove.

Something grabbed hold of her and yanked her away from being within reach of Asmodeus. Anael's body was quickly restrained, with ethereal chains wrapping around every inch of her body. She was raised off the ground and held aloft to see that Kushiel was now in Limbo as well. Uriel watched the whole thing play out with satisfaction and approached her.

"Did you think I wouldn't be prepared for this?" he asked. "You're completely finished, Anael. The Choir has no use for a treasonous bitch like you."

"Still afraid to do your own dirty work, I see," said Anael. "No matter what happens, I want you to know that I'll be the one who kills you, Uriel."

"Promises, promises," said Uriel before turning to Kushiel. "She's all yours, warden. Put her in a cell next to the Morningstar's. It's fitting for them to be so close but so far."

CHAPTER 28

Silence reigned in Gehenna. The angels were a very obedient lot for the most part, so the prison never housed more than one or two inmates at a time, and even then it wasn't for long. Most angels would end up recanting any heresies they were imprisoned for.

So when Lucifer heard sound coming from outside his cell, his curiosity got the better of him. The cell itself was little more than a box with a glass ceiling, forcing him to watch the skies of Elysium overhead, but not able to touch them. There was no door to speak of, nor any windows on the walls surrounding him.

"Kushiel, I know you're there," said Lucifer. "Whatever tortures you've planned, they won't work."

Kushiel's familiar chuckle was the first reply. "Tempting as that is, I'm not here for you just yet, Morningstar. I'm providing you with a friend."

Friend…? Lucifer's thoughts echoed that word. What friend of his would end up in Gehenna? Belial or any other demons would naturally be kept in Hell, which left only—

"Ana…?" he asked in a hushed voice.

He could hear sounds from outside his cell. Grunts of protest and then the walls rising up to box in the new prisoner. The same sounds he heard when Kushiel put him in his cell.

"I'll leave you traitors to get reacquainted. But don't despair, your torture will begin in due time." Kushiel's laughter followed him and grew softer as he left their cells.

Once the sounds of Kushiel's presence had faded, Lucifer pushed himself up against the wall of his cell and began speaking again. "Ana, is that you?"

"Yeah," said Anael.

"What are you doing here? You reported to the Choir, didn't you?"

"I did, but I felt like something was off."

Anael then proceeded to explain what had transpired since they last saw each other. How she grew suspicious of the timing of the Choir's orders from the Presence and what she'd learned of Uriel. Defying the order to remain in Elysium so she could speak with Death and then Khronus. And finally, her attempt to breach Limbo to rescue Lucifer only to learn that she'd been too late.

"After everything I said, you were still willing to risk imprisonment or even death?" asked Lucifer once the tale ended.

"Do you have to put it in such a self-aggrandizing way?" she asked.

Lucifer smiled at her attempt to make light of the situation. It didn't do anything to diminish the shame he'd felt. One could easily argue that she'd been guilty of saying awful things about him in the past, but the most-recent attacks were launched by him, even when she put herself at risk to help him. And after he failed to consider her predicament, she still went out of her way to help him, even winding up in this place.

"I'm sorry," he said.

"So am I."

Lucifer blinked in surprise. "What do you have to apologize for?"

Anael sighed. "For not trusting you long ago when you tried to tell me about the Choir."

"You believe me?"

"Partially," she said. "I'm not sure I'm ready to give up faith in the Presence, but it's become clear to me that the Choir is more interested in pursuing petty vendettas and maintaining control than fulfilling a holy mission."

"And this gift you received from Khronus?"

"Possibly a way to fix things. But we can't use it yet. We have to find the pages that contain the spell," said Anael. "I know where they are, but—"

"But first we have to get out of Gehenna," Lucifer finished.

"And Heaven," Anael added. "I don't suppose you remember how you escaped the first time?"

"Abraxas and the rebellion broke me out last time. This time, I doubt there's anyone in Heaven who will have that same compulsion," said Lucifer.

"Then what do we do?"

"I might have an idea," said Lucifer. It's a risky one, but it just might work."

"Are you going to tell me what it is?"

Lucifer's instinct was to keep it to himself. That was what he was used to. Part of his plan hinged on her reaction when the time came. He fully acknowledged that keeping secrets was how he had gotten himself into this situation. If he wanted this to be a real partnership, he would have to start trusting her.

"I want to, I do," he said with a sigh. "But I'm just going to have to ask you to trust me for now."

Anael huffed. "Same old story, huh?"

"Ana, listen to me," said Lucifer. "Once we get out of here, there won't be any more secrets between us. All I need is a little faith, for just a short time."

"That's the problem, Lucifer," she said. "I'm not sure I *have* any faith left."

It wasn't long before Kushiel returned to begin his torture of the prisoners. With a wave of his hand, one of the walls to Lucifer's cell lowered. Kushiel smiled through the hole in his mask and the chains around his arms snaked down and slithered towards the prisoner.

Lucifer attempted to put up resistance to the chains, but it was just a show for the jailer's benefit. This was all part of the Morningstar's plan and he didn't want Kushiel to have any suspicions about it. Anael contributed her part by protesting both vocally and by banging her hands against the walls of her cell.

"Your time will come, heretic," said Kushiel. "But I've waited many cycles to have the Morningstar back in my loving grasp."

Kushiel dragged Lucifer from the cell down the corridors of Gehenna. There were many other cells along the path, but these were all empty. Soon, Kushiel came to a hole that led down into darkness. His wings emerged from his back and he flew deep into the hole, pulling Lucifer behind him.

Down in the cavernous depths, Kushiel's chains released their hold on Lucifer and threw him to the stony ground. The Morningstar struck the ground and rolled a few times before coming to a stop, just as Kushiel's wings retracted. The warden landed hard, his impact sending a tremor through the ground.

"Now we can begin." Kushiel gestured with his hand and chains erupted from the wall, quickly wrapping around Lucifer's body and pulling his arms and legs until he was suspended in a spread-eagle position. "Unfurl your wings, Lucifer."

"Something tells me it won't be pleasant if I do."

"Of course it won't be, what about this made you think it would be pleasant?"

Kushiel's chains slithered closer, moving to Lucifer's back. Pincers formed at the heads of each chain and then burrowed into the Morningstar's flesh near the shoulder blades. Lucifer screamed as his wings were painfully forced free from his back.

"One feather for each day you've lived defying the will of the Presence. Such a thing would certainly seem fair," said Kushiel. "At least, for a start."

"I'm from Hell, angel. Do your worst," said Lucifer.

Kushiel's grin became almost giddy as he went about his work. White-hot pliers forged of soulfire appeared in his hand. He took hold of the first feather on Lucifer's wings. The heat of the metal sent waves of agony through the nerves in the wing. Lucifer held back the scream that threatened to burst from his lungs. Kushiel pulled on that feather. With his strength, the warden could have easily removed it quickly. But he wanted the pain to last. He wanted Lucifer to feel every millimeter of that feather being searingly pulled from its housing.

When it finally came free, there was a moment of relief and Lucifer couldn't help the cry that escaped his lips. Kushiel moved in front of the Morningstar and held up the feather with its crimson-stained quill, a drop of blood still clinging to the tip.

"That's one," said Kushiel.

He let the feather fall to the ground and went back to the wings, ready to pull out another. It was the same painful process, and Lucifer endured it, but this time allowed himself a scream. He did so because he knew it was what Kushiel wanted to hear and all of this pain and suffering was just part of Lucifer's plan.

"You're...a sadistic monster..." Lucifer finally muttered, putting the next part of his plan into action.

Kushiel smirked, taking pride in the accusation. "Your demons may think they know something of torture, but they're amateurs."

"I'm sure you could teach them a thing or two," said Lucifer. "Pity your work goes so unappreciated."

"Hah!" Kushiel's laugh echoed in the cavern. "The Choir has great appreciation for what I do."

"Then why don't they let you do it more often?" asked Lucifer. "All those empty cells I saw. Imagine what you could do with a prison full of souls."

"Unfortunately, not all angels are as blasphemous as you and your whore," said Kushiel.

"It always struck me as odd that the Choir never put you in charge of defiant souls and instead just sends them directly to Hell," said Lucifer.

"Ahh, defiance..." Kushiel spoke with a wistful tone. "I never quite agreed with the Choir's decision to cast you and the other heretics out. I pleaded to be granted custody of you all, but those prayers fell on deaf ears. Spending centuries breaking each of you…that would have been a rewarding existence."

"Oh, it wouldn't have taken that long. Angels are quite easy to break because of their innate fealty to authority. Trust me, you weren't missing anything," said Lucifer. "Now humans, on the other hand…"

Kushiel seemed intrigued. He stepped closer to Lucifer and asked, "What about humans?"

"Well, that spell I cast long ago? The one that first brought me here? It ignited the spark of free will within humanity," said Lucifer. "If you want *true* defiance, nothing beats a human. And there's no shortage of souls to torment in Hell."

Kushiel glanced down at the pliers. "I've never had a human soul."

"You would love it," said Lucifer. "But unfortunately, that's not to be."

"You don't know that," said Kushiel. "After everything I've done for the Choir, I'm sure if I requested damned souls to be sent to Gehenna…"

Lucifer scoffed. "Oh, no, I don't think so. The Choir likes having Hell around. It serves as a deterrent to defiance in humanity, which helps more humans accept Heaven's rule. That in turn shuffles more souls to Heaven and increases the Choir's power. Defiant souls wouldn't do them much good." Lucifer shook his head. "Anyway, there's no sense in continuing to tease you with something you'll never have. So, on with the torture."

"Yes, of course." Kushiel went back to the wing and took another feather in his grasp. But he hesitated before clamping down with the pliers.

"Is something wrong?" asked Lucifer. "Don't tell me that I've already gotten used to the pain."

Kushiel released the feather and walked back in front of Lucifer. "You really don't think they'll *ever* grant me a human soul?"

Lucifer frowned and shook his head. "I'm sorry, but I just don't see it in the cards."

"But in Hell, there are many of them?" asked Kushiel. "Maybe they'll allow me to work in Hell?"

"The Choir?" Lucifer laughed. "Oh of course they wouldn't allow that. They need you here as a deterrent for any angels that might rebel. You serve them better that way."

"But maybe—"

"I'm sorry, I never should have mentioned any of this. It's cruel to tell you about the pleasures of torturing human souls when you'll never be able to experience it yourself," said Lucifer. "You just need to accept your place in the celestial order."

Kushiel still hesitated. "Hypothetically, if you were to return to Hell…would you still have influence with the Infernal Court?"

"Oh, of course," said Lucifer. "The current king and I are quite close."

"And—again, hypothetically—if you were to suggest someone to lead the torture of souls…?"

"If I were to recommend someone? I'd imagine they'd be quite inclined to honor that recommendation. But I'd only recommend someone whom I felt could both do the job effectively and who did something for me in return," said Lucifer. "Hypothetically speaking, of course."

"Of course..." muttered Kushiel, staring intently at the chains that bonded Lucifer.

One by one, the links of those chains broke. The metal clattered to the stone ground and Lucifer dropped, no longer suspended in the air. His feet gently touched stone and he stood upright. Lucifer looked at Kushiel with feigned surprise.

"What are you doing?" he asked.

"Torture is my passion and I'm willing to fall to pursue that passion," said Kushiel. "I will help you escape if you help me. I want to know the pleasure of torturing human souls."

"I made this offer to you once, but you refused."

"I did," said Kushiel. "But you never mentioned the feel of torturing human souls. This...intrigues me. And just this brief torture session reminded me that once I'm done with you and Anael, I do not know when I may have another victim."

"You realize what you're doing here, don't you?" asked Lucifer. "There's no turning back."

Kushiel nodded. "I'm aware. And I'm willing to commit myself to your cause."

Lucifer smiled. "Good. But Anael comes with us."

CHAPTER 29

Kushiel kept his word. After releasing Lucifer from his chains, he took the Morningstar back to Gehenna and lowered the walls that made up Anael's cell. The angel was surprised when she saw Kushiel and Lucifer standing side by side, but her instinctive reaction was to generate a soulfire sword in her hands.

It seemed Kushiel had expected such an attack, because his reaction was swift. His chains instantly came to life, springing from his arms and restraining Anael, rendering her immobile even as she still struggled to fight against them.

Lucifer had to stop this before the display drew any unwanted attention. He unleashed a hellfire burst powerful enough to separate the two. It caused Kushiel's grip on Anael to falter, letting the chains fall from her body, but also threw the two of them apart.

"We don't have time for this," said Lucifer. "The Choir may have left Kushiel to his own devices for now, but that might not last long. I imagine it's only a matter of time before they want me brought before them in chains so they can gloat, just as they did last time."

"What's even happening right now?" asked Anael.

"Why would you stop me from killing him?"

"Because Kushiel and I had a nice little chat. He's come to realize that he chose the wrong side."

"The Morningstar has promised me human souls to torment," said Kushiel.

Anael directed an angry stare at Lucifer. "Oh *did* he now?"

Kushiel nodded, oblivious to Anael's anger at the arrangement. "Yes, he did. He said torturing a human soul is much more rewarding than a celestial. And that Hell has an abundance of souls waiting to be tortured."

Anael's anger couldn't be restrained another moment. She turned on Lucifer, bringing a soulfire dagger right to his throat. "Have you taken complete leave of your sanity?"

"Ana…" Lucifer muttered, remaining calm even when faced with a threat upon his life.

"After everything you've been through, here I thought you'd finally rise above the role the Choir put you in. And yet once again, you're playing the part of Satan."

"It's not like that…"

"How is it not?" asked Anael. "You've tempted Kushiel to betray Heaven with the promise of *torture*? How is that anything other than the kind of malicious self-dealing Devil the Choir has always tried to paint you as?"

"Shall I restrain her again, my Lord?" asked Kushiel, already falling into the familiar patterns of worship that Lucifer hated.

"No, it's fine. I can handle this," he said. "And please don't call me 'lord.' It leaves a bad taste in my mouth."

"Maybe we should see just how capable you are of *handling* me!" Anael shouted, pushing the dagger towards his throat.

Lucifer grabbed her arm and pushed her back. He wrapped his fingers around her dagger and absorbed the soulfire, his eyes crackling with fiery energy.

"Just. Relax," he said and then added in a whisper, "This situation is a lot more complicated than it seems at the moment. I need you to be calm, please. Go along with this for now and you'll see just where it's leading."

Anael's eyes were inquisitive, but her anger had softened. Her muscles relaxed and Lucifer released her. Her look spoke to her intent—she'd give him a chance, for now. But unless she saw just where this was leading and soon, there would be trouble.

"We must make haste," said Kushiel. "The Morningstar is correct in his belief that the Choir will soon demand his presence. I can transport the three of us, but we must have a destination. Shall we proceed into Hell?"

Lucifer felt Anael's glare upon him again. He gave her a reassuring look and then addressed Kushiel. "No, not yet. There are still some particulars that need to be ironed out. For now, just take us to Earth. My home."

"That is not far from Eden's gateway. It could arouse Uriel's suspicions if we three were to suddenly appear."

"It'll be fine, Kushiel. And again, it's only temporary," said Lucifer.

"As you wish. Come near."

Kushiel's wings extended to their full length. His wingspan was larger than a normal angel's, due to his far greater size. Anael and Lucifer stepped closer to Heaven's jailer, and Anael continued to fix an uncertain glare upon the Morningstar. Kushiel's feathered wings wrapped around them and in a flash of blue light, they were gone.

They materialized mere moments later near the pool

behind Lucifer's Evanston home. As soon as Kushiel un-wrapped his wings, he began scanning the skies, seeking out any sign of a threat.

"It seems we're safe for the moment, but I do not know how long that will last," he said. "If we are to truly avoid Heaven's detection, we must journey to Hell at the earliest convenience."

Lucifer moved behind Kushiel as he continued looking for potential threats. He held up his hand and something materialized in his grip. The small blade that Samedi had given him back in Limbo.

"Patience. All will be revealed in time." Lucifer glanced at Anael as he spoke those words.

"Understood. Though patience has never been my—"

As Kushiel turned to face his new master, he was greeted with Lucifer driving the small blade right into his eye. Lucifer pulled it to the side, cutting through the bone and piercing the other eye as well.

The Morningstar stepped back and watched as Kushiel collapsed to his knees, screaming in agony. His entire body glowed with bright, azure energy. It pierced through his skin, as if it were dissolving him. Where his eyes had once been was now a dark void. Kushiel's screams continued unabated until the mixture of light and darkness had consumed every last inch of his flesh.

There was a massive *boom* and an explosion of light. Once it faded, Kushiel was gone. The only sign that remained of his presence was a scorch mark on the pavement.

It took a moment for Anael to recover from the shock. Once she did, she gave Lucifer a slap on his chest. "Just what is going on?"

Lucifer recoiled from the slap and held up the blade.

"Samedi gave this to me. At the time, I wasn't sure why. If I'd realized it earlier, I could have killed Kushiel when he came for me in Limbo. Wasn't until you arrived that I realized just what it could be used for and how to escape."

"So all that talk of giving Kushiel souls to torture in Hell?" she asked.

"A lie, obviously. I figured the best way to trick him was to play the part of the Devil he thought me to be and appeal to the sense superiority and viciousness that angels pretend they don't possess," said Lucifer. "And it worked."

"And this is what you wouldn't tell me about?"

"Not for lack of trust," said Lucifer. "But my offer to Kushiel had to seem spur-of-the-moment. And for that, I needed genuine surprise from you."

"I understand. I don't like it, but I understand. Though you know that won't be the end of it," said Anael. "Asmodeus and Uriel are working together. They've already killed Beelzebub and framed Belial for it. And it won't be long before both Heaven *and* Hell realize that you've escaped. But like I said, I think I have a way to fix everything."

"Khronus and the spell," said Lucifer. "You really think we can fix everything? Remove these celestial chains that have been holding us all back since the beginning?"

"I don't know," said Anael. "But it seems we don't have much of a choice, does it?"

"Okay." Lucifer nodded. "Let's rewrite the rules then."

EPILOGUE

The Infernal Court assembled for an emergency meeting in the capital of Hell. The tower that served as the home of Luther Cross and the sole construct in the center of the seat of power was also the Court's meeting place.

Normally, there were seven seats on the Infernal Court with the eighth occupied by the King of Hell. But today, one seat remained unoccupied. Cross didn't want to preside over this meeting, yet also knew there was no choice. One of their own had been assassinated and the evidence was damning. He sat at the end of the table, listening to the arguments flying back and forth. Lilith, who was also once his consort, communicated with her expressions. Her eyes were practically screaming, "You're the King. Deal with this."

Cross stood and cried out several times for silence. No one listened, they just kept arguing past each other. His patience finally at an end, he reached into his jacket and drew the modified Magnum holstered under his arm. It had been some time since he'd had cause to use this weapon and it felt good in his hand again.

He aimed it at the ceiling and pulled the trigger. The

sound of the gun going off silenced the demons and they all turned their gaze to him.

"That's better." Cross set the gun down on the table in front of him and sat down. "Now, let's address this rationally."

"We all know what happened," said Mammon. "Beelzebub is now dead thanks to Belial, no doubt retaliation for Lucifer's conviction."

"Not as if there wasn't cause," said Vassago. "Beelzebub *did* betray the Morningstar to begin with, violated his own code."

"Only after the Morningstar betrayed all of us," added Abaddon. "Keeping secrets and then running off to Earth." The demon then realized his words could be interpreted as a backhanded attack on their current king. He turned to Cross and bowed his head. "No offense, my Lord."

Cross sighed and brushed it off. "Are we certain that Belial was responsible for this?"

"I wouldn't have thought it, but he *does* have a reputation for his temper," said Lilith. "The evidence seems quite damning."

"I'm not prepared to cast any stones until we learn the full truth," said Vassago. "Perhaps another trial is in order, one to determine Belial's guilt."

"Sssince when is the Court concerned with these ideas of due prosssess?" asked Leviathan. "What happened to your ballsss, boys?"

"We should also consider the matter of Beelzebub's realm," said Nergal. "Now that he's gone, it could quickly descend into chaos unless someone takes control."

"Who would you even nominate for that position? Not as if Beelzebub was one for cultivating potential successors," said Lilith. "He wanted nothing but sycophants."

"I know who ssshould be nominated." Leviathan stood from the table. "He'sss one of us to begin with, he recently demonstrated his talent and devotion to the Court, and he deserves the title he lost to now be ressstored."

Cross felt a sinking feeling in the pit of his stomach. He'd made that deal with Lucifer and taken over to avoid these sorts of situations, to try to bring some order to the chaos of Hell. But the more things changed, the more they stayed the same. He was quickly realizing just how ungovernable this place truly was.

"I would like to nominate Asmodeusss to take the vacant seat upon the Court."

Leviathan gestured to the doors. They opened and Asmodeus strolled in, dressed in his crisp, crimson suit and leaning on his cane. There was a devilish smile on his face as he approached the table.

"Thank you, my Mistress Leviathan, for such a beautiful introduction," said Asmodeus. "Should it please the Court, I endeavor to not only govern this territory with the same approach as the dearly departed Lord Beelzebub, but I also vow to bring his unrepentant and treasonous killer to the justice that the people so desperately cry out for."

"Are we sure of this?" asked Lilith.

"You should still your tongue," said Mammon. "Asmodeus was with us at the beginning. We fought and bled together. He served his realm and his people faithfully for eons before you came along."

"He was also instrumental in imprisoning me for the crime of falling in love with him," said Lilith. "And he was a willing servant of Thanatos's for a time."

"The first was in the service of the Court and the second was due to circumstances beyond my control," said Asmodeus. "I would never have even been in that position had I not been abandoned to Purgatory in the first place."

Cross said nothing, though his hand twitched near the gun's hilt. He couldn't express how much joy he would have felt in that moment if he'd only picked up the Magnum and blown craters in both of Asmodeus's eyes. But he couldn't do that. He had to remain stoic and allow the politics to play out.

"Then we vote," said Cross. "All those in favor of Asmodeus's return to the Court."

All hands went up, with the exception of Cross and Lilith. He sighed and then said, "All opposed?"

Those two hands alone went up. Cross lowered his arm and with a heavy heart, said the words that Asmodeus was clearly anticipating.

"The motion carries," said Cross. "Asmodeus, welcome back to the Infernal Court."

Asmodeus bowed in gratitude, the grin on his face growing as wide as it could reach. One step closer to the throne...

To be continued...

AFTERWORD

Welcome to the end of the fourth book in the *Morningstar* series and the tenth overall in the *Dark Crossroads* series that began with *Devil's Due* (well, probably twelfth if you count the two short prequels in both series). Writing a series is a tough gig. You have to keep the fans on their toes, you can't deviate too far from the formula that made them love that first book, but you also have to find a way to prevent them (and yourself) from becoming bored.

When I started the *Luther Cross* series, I more or less had a pretty rough idea of where I was going with it. There was a long, overarching story that I wanted to tell, even if I didn't know all the specifics. With *Morningstar*, it was a little looser. It wasn't so much an overarching story, but more exploring the character. And that's led into some interesting directions.

I never knew when I sat down to write *Lucifer Rising* that I would eventually get to the trial of Lucifer in Hell. All I knew at the time is that I wanted to write some stories with my take on this character, I wanted it to be unique from other versions the Devil, and I was committed to doing it over the course of five books.

Now we're at the end of Book Four and I have a pretty

good idea where I want to go next. The fifth book will be the final in this installment of the character, and it will open up a lot of possibilities in the *Dark Crossroads* universe.

I'd love to hear your thoughts on this book. Please post a review on Amazon—even just a few words expressing your opinion would be great. And though we're nearing the end of Lucifer's story, the *Dark Crossroads* universe is still ripe for exploration. So if there are any characters you're interested in becoming the focus of future series, then please drop me a line and tell me.

That's all for now, but I'll see you in the final *Morningstar* book, titled *Lucifer Forever*.

Percival Constantine
Kagoshima, Japan
September 2021

SEE HOW THE FALL BEGAN!

MORNINGSTAR
BOOK 0

LUCIFER
FALLEN

PERCIVAL CONSTANTINE

LUCIFER.PERCIVALCONSTANTINE.COM

Printed in Great Britain
by Amazon